"HELLO?"

It was Kevin's voice. "Hello," I said, all neutral, though my hand was shaking so much the phone clanked against my head.

"It's Kevin," the voice said.

"Who is it?" Tess whispered.

I gave her the "sh" sign and said, "Hi."

"Did, um," he said. "Is your . . . Did we get any homework in French over the weekend?"

"No," I said. How awkward that he would say the word *French* to me, given our history.

# if we kiss

## RACHEL VAIL

An Imprint of HarperCollinsPublishers

To Mitch, Zachary, and Liam:
I love you all over the map.

HarperTeen is an imprint of HarperCollins Publishers.

If We Kiss

Copyright © 2005 by Rachel Vail

www.epicreads.com

Library of Congress Cataloging-in-Publication Data
Vail, Rachel.
    If we kiss / Rachel Vail. — 1st ed.
        p.    cm.
    Summary: Fourteen-year-old Charlie feels guilty because
she has a crush on her best friend's boyfriend, and her loyal-
ties become even more confused when she discovers that her
mother is dating the boyfriend's father.
    ISBN 978-0-06-056916-7
    [1. Dating (Social customs)—Fiction.  2. Interpersonal
relations—Fiction.  3. High schools—Fiction.  4. Schools—
Fiction.]  I. Title.
PZ7.V1916Id 2005                            2004016979
[Fic]—dc22                                      CIP
                                                 AC

Typography by Amy Ryan
12  13  14  15  16   LP/BV   20  19  18  17  16  15  14  13  12  11
❖
Revised paperback edition, 2012

# ACKNOWLEDGMENTS

Many thanks to Amy Berkower, Abby McAden, Elise Howard, Sarah Heller, and Magda Lendzion—without you there would truly be no book and, let's be honest, an acknowledgment page with no book after it is a silly thing. When I venture out from my desk into the world, I find myself surrounded by both brilliance and kindness thanks to the good people of the Author's Guild, my cool nieces and nephews, my extraordinary friends, and especially my wonderful parents. I am indebted to readers who have shared insights with me, and to Judy Blume, for her inspiration, generosity, and friendship. A special thanks to my teachers and to my kids' teachers: I am learning from you still. And more than I can ever say, I thank the three guys I live with, for their poetry and support, their grace and their love.

In loving memory of Paula Danziger: The world is less glittery without you.

if we kiss

# one

KEVIN LAZARUS STOPPED in front of me in the hall, turned around, and asked me if I was ready for the bio quiz. While he was asking, he touched my hair. It was a strand on the front left side. He twirled it around his index finger and then let go. When he did that I couldn't remember if I was even taking bio this year. I think I may actually have said "duh." Kevin smiled and strolled into class. I sat down right there in the hall because my knees had lost their ability to support me.

I should say right up front that I don't like Kevin Lazarus. He French-kissed his last girlfriend twelve times at one party, with everybody watching (and counting), and broke up with her the next day online. He is exactly the kind of boy who has never interested me at all. But there I was on the floor outside bio.

"What are you doing on the floor?" my best friend, Tess, asked me.

"Waiting for you," I lied.

I got up and followed her into class. I should also say that at that point I had never kissed anybody. No interest, for one, and also I had some romantic ideas about how my first kiss would happen. Maybe there would be a tree above us, maybe some music would be playing. Tess thinks atmosphere is a cliché and I should just get the first kiss over with already. Since before ninth grade started, she has been trying to convince me to kiss George Jacobson.

George Jacobson is a really nice guy. One time last May during a debate in social studies, George said that, though he disagreed with my premise, it was clear that I was an independent thinker and a moral person. It was a slightly weird moment. After class, Tess said wow, George Jacobson is totally in love with you. I said no, he's just a nice guy, a gentleman. All the mothers like George. Everybody does. I like George. Good old George.

Kissing George would be like kissing my cousin.

But as I sat down at my desk in bio I realized that I was ready to kiss someone. I was suddenly, overwhelmingly, sick of waiting. I couldn't remember what exactly I'd been waiting for anymore. Tess has fallen in love with all three boys she's kissed, and she said there was no way I could possibly understand how awesome and overpowering that kind of love is without experiencing it for myself. She said it was beyond describing. Every single experience in my entire life has been describable. In fact, I have described most of them to Tess.

Kevin may be a jerk but he had scrunched his eyes when he looked at me.

Tess passed me a note: "You okay?"

I realized I hadn't started my bio quiz, hadn't even turned it over. I flipped the paper and filled in the answers. *Yes, Kevin, I did study.* I flipped it back over and picked up Tess's note again. She is my best friend. We tell each other everything. She would be happy if I finally got a crush on somebody, maybe especially Kevin Lazarus, given my rants against him. Tess is a big fan of irony.

I didn't write back, pretending instead I was still working on the bio quiz. It might be a passing weakness, I decided, like a tickle in your nose that never grows into a sneeze. I would probably stop thinking about kissing Kevin by the end of the period, I hoped, anyway, and return to my rational, self-controlled self.

Well, a week later I was almost fully back to normal. My proof is that as I was following Kevin off the bus at school the next Tuesday morning, I was deep in thought not about what would it be like to kiss him or how cute it is that the bottom bit of his hair curls up where it hits his collar, but about which is better, peanut butter with M&Ms or peanut butter with chocolate chips. At that exact moment, Kevin stopped in front of me again.

"Hey," he said.

I almost swallowed my gum.

"You walk home."

This was true. It was a statement of fact. It felt like an accusation. I started to shake my head.

"I thought you did."

Caught. What could I say? *The cover-up is worse than the crime* is what flashed through my head. "Um," I said. "Not until, um, after school."

He looked a little baffled at that, reasonably.

That broke my nervousness; I snorted a laugh. "Oh, really?" I couldn't help mocking myself. I put on a space-cadet voice and asked myself, "You mean you don't walk home immediately after getting off the bus in the morning?"

He grinned at me. "Come 'ere," he said, and grabbed my hand. The warning bell had rung. It was time to get in to school. I'm never late for school.

His hand was warm, and it was in mine.

As discreetly as possible I pressed my right fist against my mouth and stuck my gum to the back of it, just in case this was going to turn into a kissing-type thing. Even in my inexperience, I knew you are not supposed to have gum in your mouth while you kiss.

Kevin led me quickly around the side of the building, then stopped. I managed not to crash into him. I tried to look calm, cool, unperturbed. I told myself not to laugh, especially not a snorting kind of laugh. "Wha—what did—"

And then he kissed me.

There I was, pressed up against the brick wall, kissing Kevin. A decorative sticking-out brick was digging into my backbone, but I didn't want to wreck my first kiss by re-adjusting. I squeezed my eyes shut and tried to concentrate.

I wanted to be mature and focus on the kiss, but even beyond the stabbing pain in my back and the fact that the late bell had long since rung by then, I was really distracted by wondering what kind of sick French person invented this bizarre way of kissing. I'm not even supposed to share a bottle of water with anyone because of germs.

When we finished kissing I had to wipe my mouth dry. We didn't say good-bye or anything. I took my gum off the back of my hand and put it in my mouth. Luckily there was still some mint flavor left because the taste in my mouth was a little mildewy. I thought, maybe this is what Kevin's mouth always tastes like—Ew. To keep myself from gagging, I tried to concentrate on the mintiness and also on the fact that it was the kind of gum that supposedly kills the germs that cause bad breath so, well, maybe it could kill whatever germs Kevin might've given me. Which made me that much more queasy.

We started walking toward the entrance of school. I let my hand dangle in case he wanted to hold it again but apparently he didn't.

I picked up the pace as we got to the door and, crossing the lobby, scanned the halls for Tess. She wasn't there.

Surprisingly I felt a little relieved. I wanted to not tell her all about it for a few minutes. I wasn't sure yet whether it had been a describable or indescribable experience. My first kiss. Well, it was disgusting, but I liked it. Uh-oh. Describable?

I heard Kevin's footsteps behind me, coming closer. Maybe the experience was still going on, and that's why I wasn't sure. We were approaching the corner near the office and Kevin was catching up to me. I slowed down. Should I spit out my gum again, in case he was coming back for more?

# two

JUST AS KEVIN caught up to me and I spat my gum into my hand, Mr. Herman rounded the corner and said, "Charlotte, Kevin, follow me."

Mr. Herman is the head ninth grade teacher. He scares me because he's so hairy. Everybody calls him Mr. Hair-Man. Not to his face, of course. I think it's mean but I call him that, too, and you have to be really careful when you talk to him, to make sure you say Mr. *Herman*. One kid supposedly made a mistake and called him Mr. Hair-Man a few years ago and got suspended for a week, which goes on your permanent record.

So there I was, totally busted, walking down the hall with Mr. Hair-Man between me and Kevin, and I almost started to crack up from the adrenaline and also because by mistake my gum-filled hand brushed against the Hair-Man's paw. It took me all the way until Hair-Man's office to calm myself down. He made Kevin wait on the chair outside his office. Divide and conquer, I guess.

"Charlotte," he said. He is the only person who calls me Charlotte except for my father and sometimes my mother when she's pretending to be really mad.

"Yes," I said, dropping the gum wad into his trash.

"Sit down."

I sat down, feeling like quite the obedient puppy. My right leg was shaking, bopping up and down, like my father's does. I wiped my sticky palm on my jeans.

"You're late."

"Yes."

"Look out my window."

"What?"

He indicated the window with his furry hand. To stop looking at the paw, I went to the window. There, just to my right, was the spot on the wall with the decorative sticking-out brick where I had just gotten my first kiss. Uh-oh.

I did not want to turn around.

"Not only were you and your boyfriend deliberately tardy, you were kissing on school property, right outside my office window."

*My boyfriend?*

Then he went on to tell me that kissing was not a proper thing to do on school property, especially when we were supposed to be in homeroom. I nodded, still thinking, *"you and your boyfriend"* until the Hairball interrupted my pleasant little moment by saying, "I'm going to have to call your mother."

"My mother?"

The shaking spread from my leg to the rest of me. Suddenly there were tears running down my face. I don't even know why. It's not like my mother would even be so mad, though she'd probably feel compelled to give me a Talk, which really is torture. But more than that, I was just coping with a lot at once. Mr. Herman was not exactly the first person I wanted to share my first-kiss moment with.

Anyway, I just kind of suddenly started bawling right there in the office. The worst part was that Mr. Hair-Man looked as surprised as I felt by the drama of my reaction, and started pulling out Kleenex and handing them to me one at a time with his hairy hand. He came around his desk and sat on the edge, telling me he wasn't trying to be mean to me.

Yeah, well, your Nobel Peace Prize is in the mail.

I said I was sorry and could I please go to the bathroom.

He said, "By all means," which is good because I had a sudden urge to ask him what he thought it meant if my "boyfriend" held my hand before our first kiss but not after—does it mean I did something wrong? Does it mean I am a bad kisser? It's my first time! Maybe I will improve with practice! Can't a person ever get a break? I hesitated briefly at the door; despite how hairy he is, maybe he's kissed, sometime, in his life. Ew. But maybe, I thought, he'd have some insight or advice from the male point of view, if he has. Luckily my one functional brain cell fired again and propelled me out the door before I could get into a conversation that would surely freak me out and probably the Hair-Man, too.

I dashed past Kevin and spent the rest of the period in the stall crying. It wasn't just Mr. Herman, it was so many things. I'll never have another first kiss. When I'm thirty-eight and someone mentions the words *first kiss*, this day is what I will have to think of, and it will be all tied up with Hair-Man. No music, no tree, just a painful decorative brick. My throat felt sore; I didn't know whether from crying or from Kevin's germs.

Oh, man, how gross. His germs.

Kevin Lazarus. So much for being a pure person. Now I was the same as Darlene Greenfudder, the one who Kevin kissed the twelve times. My boyfriend? I didn't even know if Kevin liked me. At all. Or if I liked him, for that matter.

What if I am a terrible kisser?

What if kissing is like gymnastics and if you don't start really young, you'll never be good at it?

When the bell rang I tried to go out but then I saw Tess. She asked me what was wrong and I instantly started bawling again. It was like throwing up—beyond my ability to control and basically convulsing my stomach, turning me inside out. We rushed back into the bathroom. Darlene Greenfudder followed us in, too. I was literally gulping for air, which was so weird because I did not even know what I was so upset about. I mean, I hadn't gotten in that much trouble, really.

"What happened?"

"Hair-Man," I said, sniffing. "He busted me."

"For what?" Darlene's been busted so many times; she looked psyched to have company.

I swallowed. "Tardiness," I said.

Tess cracked up. I started laughing, too. That was so the least of it.

"What?" asked Darlene.

"You are dead," Tess mocked. "Tardiness? Your mom is going to kill you." Tess is always giving me crap about how lucky I am that my mother is so laid back and cool. Her parents probably *would* have a fit about tardiness.

"My mom would probably be psyched if one day the worst thing I did was tardiness," Darlene said. "That means late, right?"

I smiled sympathetically at her. "Yeah."

"If you get grounded and want to know how to climb out your window, you should call me."

"Thanks." Darlene is not one of my closest friends, but she's sort of trying to shift over from the smokers to me and Tess and Jennifer Agnihotri. I don't mind. I don't look down on someone just because of how much makeup she wears. But I wasn't about to share the news about my first kiss with her.

We got ourselves off the floor then, and after I washed my face, we all headed to class. I figured I would tell Tess later about *why* the tardiness had happened, when I got her alone.

# three

TESS WAS RUSHING off to try out for chamber choir
after school. I grabbed her and whispered, "I have to tell you
something."

Tess nodded, but started rushing down the hall, with her
pinkie and thumb spread like a phone beside her ear, and
yelled, "I'll call you."

"Call my cell," I said.

"Yeah. Wish me luck!"

"Me, too!" I yelled back.

She spun around and blew me a kiss, then ran toward
the stairs.

I walked home through the woods. Some small dumb
part of me wondered if Kevin would meet me, walk me
home, talk with me about what Hair-Man had said, maybe

hold hands again, maybe even kiss some more. He knew I walked home, obviously. I kind of lingered at the entrance to the path, but after the buses pulled away it became clear he was gone. I walked home alone, telling myself it was much better this way—I like my time alone and also I was out of gum so maybe my breath would be not as fresh this time. It doesn't mean anything, I told myself, that he asked me if I walked home and then did nothing about it. It doesn't necessarily mean I turned him off during the kiss.

It could mean some other thing. It could.

That's what I was telling myself when the back door of my house swung open and my mother announced, "Charlotte Reese Collins! I can*not* believe! How in the world?"

I walked into the house. Our neighbors aren't that near but Mom can sure project.

"Kissing against the wall? Against the wall?"

Like the big issue was the location. Like if it had been in the cafeteria, no problem. I left my shoes in the hall and went to the kitchen to get a can of Coke.

"Mr. Herman called me at work," Mom said. "I was in a meeting with Blumstein, and Mr. Herman called, said it was urgent, and then, loudly, proceeded to give me details of my daughter, Charlie, of all people, tardy because of kissing *against the wall.*"

"Of all people?" I sat on a stool at the breakfast bar and popped open the can. "Thanks a lot." My second conversation about my first kiss was so far going about as well as the first.

"Well," Mom said, reopening the fridge and getting herself a Coke, too. "Was it that nice George?"

The Coke was too bubbly; it made my eyes water. I rested my head on the breakfast bar and let my mother talk. *Appropriate times, some things are private, love can be beautiful when blah, blah, blah.* Exactly what I had been trying to avoid.

When I thought we'd both had enough of that, I headed upstairs. Mom followed me all the way up the stairs to the bathroom, talk, talk, talking, and then sat on the floor while I threw two Tylenols down my throat and chased them with the dregs of my Coke. I leaned against the sink and eventually slid down the cabinet onto the floor. Mom was still lecturing me so I clamped my head between my knees and folded my arms over my head. *Reputation, self-respect. Why should he buy a cow?*

"What?"

My mother shook her head and said it was an expression her mother used to use, never mind.

"Why should *who* buy a cow?" We live in the suburbs. Nobody has a cow.

"Nobody. George. So was it George?"

"Am I the cow?"

"Oh, Charlie," Mom groaned. "Forget the cow. Do you understand what I'm telling you?"

The only unexpected thing she had said was *why should*

*he buy a cow,* and it was obvious she wasn't going to explain that. I had to escape. So I said all the old standbys: "Yes, thank you, I'm sorry."

Mom gave me a kiss on the hair, and I was free to go. Hallelujah. I think we were both relieved.

When I got to my room, I turned on my computer right away, thinking about Kevin. Did I really make out with Kevin Lazarus? A lot of my friends were online, but not Tess yet. And not Kevin, either. Darlene wanted to know if my party Friday night was still on. Poor Darlene. I wrote back that luckily my mother hadn't thought of canceling it, and actually let me off with just a Tardiness Talk. She IM'ed that if I wanted she'd come over sometime and teach me how to climb out my window, in case I got grounded sometime. I typed *Thanks, GTG.*

I just didn't have the energy for everybody's stressful conversations online, for once, so I did my homework. Mom and I had an uncivilized dinner, which means we can read during it, and then I went upstairs to check the computer again.

On my way up, I was thinking how unfair or at least ironic it was that I, of all people (as my mother so generously pointed out), would have gotten in trouble for kissing at school when I am such a prude. But by the top landing I was thinking maybe it was worth it.

I can't say the tongue part was good. It may just be one of those things you have to get used to, like other French stuff. Cream sauces. Hairy armpits. My mother went to France for a year in college and after a few months she got used to those things and the weird way you have to say *R* sounds. I don't know. I don't like French toast, either. I eat cereal Saturdays while my mother dips bread in scrambled eggs and fries it into a gloppy mess. She says she didn't like it when she was my age but she learned to, later. So there's a chance I'll learn to like the stuff. On the other hand, I may turn out to be a person who doesn't acquire tastes, or who is anti-French. That's a thing, I think, like a political position of some kind. But even beyond politics, there are probably plenty of adults who don't enjoy French toast. Or French kissing.

Actually, it is absolutely nauseating to imagine any adult I know enjoying French kissing.

I lay down on my bed and wiggled my tongue around in my mouth, to try to re-create the moment. It didn't work. I folded it over and sucked but that still wasn't exactly it. On the other hand, my tongue started feeling too big for my mouth. What a weird thing a tongue is.

But other than that and the germs, there was something nice about the moment of the kiss. I'm not sure if it was pressing the front of me into the front of Kevin, or if it was his hands gripping my shoulders, or his warm breath on my cheek. I closed my eyes and tried to remember all the details. I think part of what I liked was the way my neck stretched as my head bent back. I tipped my chin up toward the ceiling.

Not sure why that felt so good, but it really did. I touched my neck. Now there's a part of me I never particularly noticed before. My neck. The skin was soft. Maybe I have a nice neck. Maybe next time we kiss, Kevin will touch my neck and fall in love with me because of it. I resolved to do neck-stretching exercises every night, in hopes.

I wondered if Tess had a nice neck, too; I couldn't help it. She looks a little like me, only prettier. I don't say that to put myself down. I am perfectly happy with myself and everything. It's just that we look a lot alike, Tess and I, to the point where substitute teachers used to get us confused, and I started wearing mismatched socks every day to have a *thing*. Tess wears plain white. It's not that we're identical at all; if you wanted to say which is which, you would say that Tess has a better smile and is more fun than I am. Probably, though I honestly have never noticed particularly, her neck is more beautiful, too.

Caring about looks is petty and dumb, and fun is not everything, but still, I made a wish that my neck would please be better than Tess's.

I got my cell phone and called Tess. Without even saying hello Tess said, "I got into chorus."

"Great," I said. "They told you right away?"

"Everybody got in," she said. "All three of us. They wanted ten."

"Oh," I said. "Well, congratulations anyway."

"Thanks." She laughed. "So? Did you get a Talk?"

"Yeah, actually."

"Really?"

"Not kidding."

"That's so weird. I can't even imagine your mother knowing how to give a Talk. Are you sure?"

"She was channeling my grandmother."

"Oh, dread," said Tess, who has met my grandmother. "Well, so, how was it?"

"Boring," I said. "Although, she said something about buying a cow."

"To punish you?"

"I think it was a figurative cow."

"Ah," Tess said. "I think that's a tradition among the Amish, giving a figurative cow as punishment for tardiness."

"Maybe we're converting," I said.

"Bummer. There's my call-waiting. It was so funny, I completely screwed up my audition, and they still—oh, man, it's my mother calling. Should I pick up?"

"She hates when you don't."

"I know. I want to tell you about . . . I better get it. She's already mad at me for stealing her lip gloss, which I didn't, technically. Wish me luck."

"Tess—"

She had already hung up.

I closed my eyes and lay down on my bed again, getting back to Kevin and remembering. Part of my brain was warning *don't try to describe each tiny detail or you'll ruin the indescribableness*, but the rest of my brain couldn't help pushing ahead, going over and over that moment, putting it into words so I'd never lose my grip on it. It was kind of hard to figure out, because at the same time I also wanted to lose control of my emotions. I really did, like Tess has done when she has fallen in love.

Might he have been sort of humming? I definitely didn't notice humming at the time of the kiss, but as I lay in my bed trying to relive it, I kept hearing this little sighing hum in my mind, the second before his lips touched mine. I am ninety to ninety-five percent sure Kevin hummed, or else sighed. It was more of a sigh, I think. Nobody ever told me about that part. Maybe that's what always happens. The boy sighs a private little hum-sigh only the about-to-be-kissed girl can hear. Or maybe that was unique to Kevin and me, and our kiss. Oh, that has to be the most romantic thing. I hope I wasn't supposed to make a private noise, too. No, Tess definitely would have told me if I had to make a noise. She would've made me practice.

I pulled the blankets up to my nose and tried to imitate Kevin's sound myself. I flipped over and pressed myself against the mattress, pretending I was kissing Kevin instead of my Red Sox pillow. Now I get it, I thought, now that I've had the experience myself: I am falling, almost indescribably, in love.

# four

THE NEXT MORNING I woke up terrified: *What if he's not in love with me?* I could make a complete fool of myself, if that's the case, or if he *thinks* I'm in love with him, because what if that whole kissing thing was no big deal to him, just a Tuesday morning pretty much like any other?

So obviously the only reasonable plan of action was to wait and see how he was going to act. I pretended not to see him by the lockers, even when I doubled back pretending I had forgotten something to give him a second chance to make his move.

My face was so hot, my ears burned as I passed him going into bio. He didn't ask me if I had studied, he didn't twirl my hair, but he was standing in that same spot. That might mean something.

He didn't look at me at all.

I made a deal with myself during bio. If he shows any indication that there's something between us, like if he talks to me or squinches his eyes while looking at me—okay, if he looks at me—it means I didn't imagine the kiss and I can get excited, tell Tess, plan to kiss him again, no, make out with him at my party Friday night. If not, it never happened, and nobody ever needs to know. Well, nobody besides me and Kevin. And my mother, who doesn't know it was Kevin. And Mr. Hair-Man. But nobody else needs to know, unless Kevin gives me even the smallest sign that he likes me. Or that he remembers it happened. Or that he has any clue who the heck I am.

Nothing.

"You sure you're okay?" Tess asked as we headed back inside after lunch. "You're even spacier than usual today."

"It never happened," I answered.

"What never happened?" she asked.

"Um," I said. "What?"

"You said it never happened. What didn't?"

"Lots of things," I answered. "Time travel, immortality, calorie-free chocolate . . ."

"You need a hobby," Tess said.

"Basketball tryouts are today," Jennifer offered, thankfully diverting the attention from me. I have to learn not to blurt stuff out if I am going to be a girl who kisses and does not tell. Tell what? It never happened.

"She can't even dribble," Tess pointed out. "Anyway, Charlie hates organized activities."

"I only like disorganized activities," I said.

George laughed. He was right behind me; I don't know for how long.

"What?" I asked. He always startles me.

"If you like disorganized activities, you should join marching band."

"That bad, huh?"

"Worse."

"Too bad I don't know how to play an instrument."

"Doesn't stop the rest of us," he said, and turned around to go into the boy's room.

"He so loves you," Tess whispered for the billionth time. "When are you going to get over yourself and just kiss him?"

"No interest," I said, getting my books out of my locker.

Next to me, Jennifer shrugged. She has never had a boy-friend. "Me either," she said.

"Yeah," Tess said, "but you hate boys. Charlie doesn't."

"I only hate boys who cry when they lose," Jennifer said. "I just have no interest in kissing them."

"Same here," I agreed. "Although I don't mind if they cry when they lose."

As we headed toward English, it occurred to me that Jennifer is now the only one of the three of us who hasn't kissed. Although it never happened, it really did happen—I have kissed a boy. Bleh. Sometimes it's easier being around Jennifer than Tess, even though Tess is my best friend.

Kevin was hanging out by the doorway of English class. I turned away from him. What, is that like his cool thing? He lurks in classroom doorways choosing which girl to slay? Please. Right then I actually believed myself, that I had no interest in kissing or boys or romance or love or any of that. Maybe I could learn to dribble, I thought. Maybe I would try out for basketball and become a sporty girl. Maybe I'm not so clumsy and spacey. There's more to me, obviously, than people knew. I could be capable of anything, maybe.

Feeling so strong and sporty, I glanced back at Kevin. He was looking at me, but turned away as soon as I caught him and kind of slunk to his seat, like I had been the one dissing him.

Well, maybe I was. And if so, good for me.

Being tough like that definitely seemed like the right thing to do, but deep down I knew that I really was too clumsy to dribble a basketball and also that I still loved him. Kevin was the first boy I ever French-kissed and that is special; it means something. Tess thinks I subconsciously love George but the truth is I forget about George all day until he pops up behind me. Kevin was crowding out absolutely everything. I felt all twitchy and sweaty and cold and like my heart was beating way too fast for just sitting in English class. There is no way love could be any more intense without physically injuring a person.

Besides, French kissing somebody you don't even love would be pretty slutty. And I am not a slut; I am a prude. Well, I was. Maybe I am both a slut *and* a prude. What a mess. No, I think you have to choose one or the other. Definitely. Otherwise, how would you know how to behave in any given situation? The thing is, now that I have surprised myself, it's impossible for me to anticipate what I might do next.

I sat there sweating and hyperventilating through English class, hoping that Kevin wasn't grounded either and that he would come to my party Friday night. I thought maybe we would get together at the party. Maybe we would kiss thirteen times and everyone would see. He could ask me out at the beginning of the party and then it would be only slightly slutty to kiss like that.

The first kiss, I decided, didn't really count. Maybe it actually hadn't even happened; maybe I truly had imagined the whole thing. I used to have a very strong imagination when I was a little kid, or so my mother says; maybe I still do. But even if not, even if it actually did happen in reality, it didn't have any ramifications. It didn't change my life like a real first kiss should.

I wanted to kiss him again. If we kiss again, I decided, it will be better, and more romantic, and everybody will know, and nothing will ever be the same after it.

# five

FRIDAY AFTERNOON, Tess and Jennifer and I decorated my basement. We had thought about a swim party but
the Association wouldn't let us use the Clubhouse pool in
the evening. Apparently it is not for the "enjoyment of the
community" on a Friday night.

No big deal. We changed it from a water theme to an
Autumnal Equinox Harvest theme and hung up pictures of
corn that Jennifer drew. We thought we were pretty witty
with that, you know, corn, corny. Whatever. Nobody seemed
to get it but us. I heard a few Pop-Tarts whispering that it felt
like a seventh grade party. I was slightly tempted to tell them
*that is the point you pseudosophisticated, don't have your driver's*
*license yet either, stuck up, should go home if you don't like it prigs,*
but I restrained myself and smiled knowingly, hostessily. It is

the depth of loserdom to stand at a party whispering that it is an uncool party. In my opinion. Hello—this party is *intentionally* corny. You are standing under a corn cob, for heaven's sake.

Kevin finally showed up just after eight. His father brought him. We ignored each other. I wasn't nervous. Plenty of time.

I went up to the kitchen at around quarter of nine to get more pretzels. My friends and I always used to laugh at the Pop-Tarts, which is what we call the flirty girls because they are both Pop(ular) and Tart(y). Pop-Tarts would never eat a thing at a party unless it was a mint. Bunch of doinks. I love pretzels and eat them at any opportunity, or did. I still had never actually flirted, but I decided I might, or more. So for the first time ever at a party I didn't eat anything. I wanted to keep my breath minty, in case Kevin and I started to flirt and ended up kissing.

A few parents were hanging around the kitchen with my mother, including, I noticed, Kevin's father. Mom took out a bag of pretzels for me and whispered, "You guys aren't playing spin the bottle, are you?"

"Oh, please!" I took an Altoid from Mom's tin on the counter. I was so hungry.

"It came up in conversation," she whispered, opening the bag. She poured the pretzels into the bowl and flattened down the heap in the center. "Are you having fun?"

I nodded, wondering if she was going to quiz me on why

I was having fun and who I liked. I'd noticed when Kevin walked in that my mother was watching him. I wondered if she knew that it was really him I had been kissing in the hall and that it was him I liked. I wondered if she thought he was the cutest boy at the party, the best one.

"Good," she said. I could tell she was waiting for more information but I wasn't about to hang around in the kitchen the whole party gossiping with my mother. Is that what she wanted? Too bad. Just because I got caught kissing once at school doesn't give my mother the right to start supervising my life like I'm a ten-year-old. I was about to tell her she can trust me or not, I don't care, and that it's my life and my tongue and I can do whatever I want with both of them.

"Are you angry about something?" Mom asked.

"No!" I pulled the bottom of my shirt to stretch it and said, "I just don't want to waste . . . I gotta go."

"It seems like a good party," Mom said. "Have fun."

I gritted my teeth. Sometimes lately she is so incredibly annoying. She held out the box of Altoids. I took another one, said "Thanks," and went back downstairs with the bowl of pretzels.

Kevin was making out with Tess.

Her arms were around him and her tongue was in his mouth. My wrists felt numb. I dropped the bowl of pretzels. It was plastic so it didn't shatter, just rolled around a little on the tiles, making whirling sounds. I meant to run upstairs

27

but I couldn't get my legs working. Everybody was staring at me. Well, everybody except the kissers.

Darlene started picking up pretzels and putting them back in the bowl.

When Tess finally stopped kissing Kevin in the middle of my playroom, she saw my face and ran over to me. She dragged me to the downstairs bathroom.

"What's wrong?" she asked.

"Nothing," I said. "I just . . . I was startled. That's all." I couldn't look at her. I started picking at the grouting from between the floor tiles. "I just, I came into the room, and you were making out with . . . I just . . ."

"You were startled? How do you think I felt? You threw a bowl of pretzels at me."

"No, I didn't." I had to laugh. Her face was so shocked. "I just dropped it."

"A pretzel hit me in the ankle."

"Are you injured?"

"My lawyer will contact yours."

"Okay. Fair enough."

"Why were you so startled?" she asked. "That was really embarrassing, having you react like that."

"Sorry." I rested my chin on my knees. "I don't know."

"You think he's a jerk, don't you?"

"Yeah," I admitted. "And a slut."

"Yeah," she agreed. "Though so am I."

"No, you're not."

"Compared to you, I mean," she said.

"Oh."

"But can I tell you? Kevin kisses a little, I mean, not slobbery at all, but a little hard, like he presses against your chin a little too hard, and his tongue . . ."

I stood up. I did not want to talk about Kevin's tongue. "What?"

"I'm thirsty," I said.

"Okay." She stood up, too. "You sure get twitchy talking about kissing. I think deep down you really want to, if you'd just ever let yourself."

"Let's continue my analysis later, okay, Dr. Freud?" I suggested. "After we find some sodas."

No cans were left in the basement, and Kevin wasn't there anymore, either. I was clenching my teeth to keep from asking Tess if by any chance she thought his mouth tasted mildewy at all, and if that was usual with boys' mouths. We went up the stairs, me staying behind her, my jaw clenched tight.

Kevin was at the back door with his father, who was still talking to my mother. I wanted to be a good host but I knew that if my mother saw me she would call me over to say thank you for coming or some horrendous thing like that, so I whispered quickly to Tess that I had a headache and went around the other way, through the kitchen to the front stairs.

I did have a headache, actually, but when Mom came up a little later I told her I could handle it, please leave me alone, I am fourteen years old, I know how to cope with a headache by myself, believe it or not. I got in bed and pretended to read, wondering if my best friend or at least my mother was planning to come in and check on me at all, see if I had a fever. Nobody did.

I didn't go down to help clean up, despite Mom's suggestion through my closed door. Tess and Jennifer were sleeping over anyway; from their laughter I could tell they were very obviously enjoying themselves so they didn't need my assistance. At midnight, they tiptoed in and inflated the air mattresses. Usually when they sleep over all three of us sleep down on the floor, but I stayed in my bed, alone, throwing myself my own private little pity party.

# six

I SPENT THE whole week thinking about him all the time, Kevin, Kevin, Kevin—even though in gym on Wednesday he was running in this really peculiar way, all uncoordinated and doofy, his feet circling out to the sides. Even that didn't shut me down on him. It was very strange, especially when I started thinking that I shouldn't think about him so much and I didn't know how not to, anymore.

So what I did was this: I asked George out. Online. He said yes.

I thought it might help set me right again but so far, no. I just feel worse about myself, treacherous in so many ways. Tess is all happy for me, and George has started meeting me after each class to walk me to my next one. Good old George, such a gentleman. It would be so much easier if I could get myself to love him instead.

I was also really wishing I had told Tess about the Kevin kiss. Now too much time had passed so I would have to carry this secret to my grave. All my other take-it-to-the-grave secrets are *with* somebody, mostly with Tess. I never kept one to myself before, which I used to worry made me shallow and transparent. But actually an alone-secret is mostly (though not completely) a stressful and isolating thing to have, it turns out.

The regular phone rang last night. When I picked it up and said, "Hello?" the voice that said "Hi" back was Kevin's.

"Hi," I said.

*Kevin.*

Finally, I thought. Finally he's calling me, after all my wishing. After I asked out George. Uh-oh. Why was he calling me? Maybe it just took making him jealous? Is that what I had to do all this time? Use George? Is Kevin really that shallow? My heart was pounding. *He likes me after all,* I thought. He does, he must, or why would he be calling? Why would he make out with Tess, though, if he likes me? Maybe he was trying to make *me* jealous? Am I that shallow? What if he's calling to ask me out and I say I can't, I'm going out with George and he says oh, okay, forget it then? And I've missed my chance forever? Oh, my head was spinning.

"So how did it go?" he asked.

It? How did what go? I had no idea what he was talking about. I tried to remember if anything other than brooding about him and checking my computer to see if he had by any chance written to me was happening in my life. He sounded so confident that he was asking a reasonable question that I thought maybe there was something momentous that I was supposed to have done that day, something maybe I had forgotten because thoughts about Kevin himself had just crowded the important thing right out of my mind. I didn't want to seem like the idiot I felt like and say what are you talking about? So instead I said, casually, "Fine."

"Great," he said. "Blumstein liked it?"

Blumstein is my mother's boss.

"Huh?" I said.

"Elizabeth?"

Elizabeth is my mother. So I said, "Kevin?"

"No," said—I swear—Kevin.

"Hold on," I said. "Mom!"

She picked up. My heart was still thumping a few minutes later when Mom yelled from the kitchen, "Charlie, it's George!"

"No, it's not," I yelled back.

"Yes it is," she yelled back.

An impasse. I didn't know who that was, that person who sounded exactly like Kevin, but it definitely was not George. "No, it is not," I said.

"He called on call-waiting!"

"I'll call him back," I yelled. "You can finish. Who are you talking to?"

"I'm done," she said, coming up the stairs with the portable. She thrust it toward me and whispered, "He's so cute."

"Who?"

She pointed at the phone.

"Kevin?"

"George!" She made a face like why was I being so thick, and left.

I looked at the phone and thought about that for a second, if George was cute or not. I realized I didn't know if he was or wasn't. It seemed beside the point.

"Hello?" I was not sure who would answer.

It was George, just George, just calling to say hi. I told him some guy had called before and thought I was my mom. George said, "Yeah, you do sound alike, actually. Probably the structure of your larynx, don't you think?"

I said, "You want to watch TV over the phone?"

He said, "Sure," so we did for a while.

"It's all so fleeting," I said, as the TV announcer promised to be right back after a short break.

He didn't say anything right away so I wasn't sure if maybe I had just imagined blurting such a random thing out loud. A commercial for particularly greasy-looking hamburgers came on. I had to look away.

"Yeah," George said. "You're right. It is all so fleeting." So I guess he'd heard me.

I wasn't sure whether to feel relieved or mortified. "You

know what I mean?" I asked him.

"Not really," he answered. "Fleeting?"

"Forget it."

"I won't," he said. "Tell me."

I wasn't even sure what I meant myself. "I don't know." I picked up the newspaper I'd been sitting on and pointed at it. "Like this," I said.

"Hamburgers?"

"No," I said. "Not on the TV. The weather."

"Well, yes," he said. "Weather is definitely more fleeting than hamburgers. But . . . "

"Never mind." I watched a commercial for khaki pants, grateful the hamburger had gone away. The pants music was so annoying, I pressed mute. "The weather *report*."

"The weather report is fleeting?" George asked.

"Yes," I said. "It is. There it is, up on the top corner of the paper, and it's like the only thing some people ever read of the news. Right?"

"That's true," said George. "My dad."

"Right. Okay. It's so vitally important, the only thing on people's minds, and then the next day they don't even care what the weather was before; they're on to the vitally important question of what is the weather *today*. Unless there's, like, a major hurricane or something, it is totally unimportant and unmemorable what the weather was like last Tuesday, or a year ago Thursday."

Pause. "True."

"Don't you find that depressing? And, like, disconcerting?"

Pause. "You're in a weird mood."

I dropped the paper. "It's a metaphor for my life," I mumbled.

"The weather report?"

"I just . . . It's like you can't hold on . . ."

"The weather report is a metaphor for your life?"

"Fine. You're right," I told George. "I'm in a weird mood. I should go get my homework done before I . . . before I . . . I don't know."

"Before you scatter showers?"

"Exactly."

"Okay. See you tomorrow," said George.

"Yeah?" I asked, but he'd already hung up.

I do like George, I guess. There's nothing not to like. I feel bad for him, though. He has this idea of me that he likes a whole lot more than he'd ever like the actual, secret, horrible me. He thinks I have values and standards and morals, that I'm "mature," that I'm "deep." But I'm not the person he and my mother think I am, or at least I'm not anymore.

Because the sad fact is, if that really had been Kevin on the phone earlier, calling to ask me out, I would've dumped George in one hot second.

# seven

"SO HERE'S THE thing and tell me the truth," Tess said as we were walking to the lockers. "Promise?"

"Sure." When people say "Tell me the truth," I usually lie. It is because, well, it is because I am not a truthful person for one thing, but it is also because they are usually asking me something about which it will be in some way hard to tell the truth. You wouldn't say, for instance, "Tell me the truth: Do you have math third block?" You would just say, "Do you have math third block?" Because whether you do or don't have math third block is not a difficult truth to reveal.

"Okay." Tess took a dramatic breath. "Do you hate Kevin Lazarus?"

The truth? Do I hate Kevin?

"I don't hate him," I answered truthfully.

"But do you like him?"

I could twist it around and say I was sort of being truthful in that I don't like him; I am in love with him. I don't like him; I am totally, paralyzingly obsessed with him. But in the privacy of my own head, I have to admit that I knew that what she was asking was not, do you have mildly positive *as opposed to* chart-bustingly positive feelings for Kevin. My best friend was asking if I liked him the way I actually did very much and at every waking moment *like him.*

"No," I said. "Definitely not." What could be worse than admitting you like someone who obviously doesn't like you?

"I think," she said. "I think I do, maybe."

Okay, that answered my *what could be worse* question. In response, I very articulately dropped my books.

It would have been bad enough if I had simply dumped all my books out of my arms, scattering them across the hall, but no. In case that remarkably low level of coordination looked too suave, I tripped over them. Well, I stepped on my social studies notebook while trying to catch my bio text in midair, not realizing how hard it is to catch a book that weighs more than a toddler as it speeds toward the ground. It smashed me in the wrist, and, off-balance as I was from standing not on firm ground but on shaky history (notes), I slid. The only positive thing is that I didn't smash into the Hair-Man himself, because between me, figure skating on my books, and the head ninth grade teacher, sitting furrily at his desk, was—a wall. A wall that I crashed into, full-force, with my head.

Tess helped me up. "You okay?"

"Mild concussion." I avoided making eye contact by gathering up my stuff as hordes of kids stomped over us. Tess helped, too. She really is a good friend.

She's the one who managed to get most of my stuff and restore it to some semblance of order, actually. "Thanks," I said, taking it from her.

"No problem."

We walked toward our lockers.

"Why," I had to ask. "Why did you think, what made you think I liked Kevin?"

"No," she said. "I know you don't *like* him. I just hoped, maybe, that you, like, didn't think he was a complete jerk."

"Oh," I said. So she wasn't asking at all what I'd thought she was asking. It wasn't that she thought I secretly liked him. It was only about her. Oh. I wasn't sure if I should feel relieved or insulted, or lonely. "No," I said. "I think he's an incomplete jerk."

Tess laughed. She has a really wicked laugh.

I smiled, then pretended to focus on my combination lock. If Kevin liked me at all he wouldn't have made out with my best friend in my basement less than a week after making out with me. Anyway, why would I like someone who would do that?

"Are you mad at me for something?" Tess asked. "Tell me the truth, Charlie, seriously."

*Tell me the truth.*

"I'm not mad at you, Tess."

"Promise? Because you seem pretty annoyed today."

I dumped my books into my locker. "I just, if anything, I'm not sure why you would like him. Kevin Lazarus?" I really liked saying his name. How sick is that?

"You're right," Tess said. Then she banged her head against a locker. "I don't know why either. But . . ."

"But you like him."

Tess nodded.

I nodded back, in an understanding way. Of course, unfortunately, I did understand.

"I'm an idiot," she said. "I know. So—but, do you think you could try to find out, from Kevin, if he . . ."

"I'll ask him before bio," I said, not needing any more information or inspiration for acrobatic routines.

"Okay," she said, still scanning my face for the truth. "Thanks."

I waited in the same spot he had been in the day he touched my hair and hurled me deep into the insanity of love. Why I had ever thought love might be a desirable thing to fall into, I could not begin to remember. Is anything a good thing to fall into?

"Kevin." It felt romantic in my mouth.

He looked at me with those unbelievably blue eyes.

I took a breath, thinking, *she is my best friend.*

Kevin came closer, close to me like the day he twirled my hair. He could have touched that strand of hair again if he wanted to. He apparently didn't want to. I twirled it myself, not hinting but, well, okay, hinting.

He looked right into my eyes. I looked back but only for a second, then looked down at my feet. What do you know? There they were, right at the bottoms of my ankles, same as last time. Still wearing one pink sock, one green.

I glanced up again, realizing he was probably getting impatient with me. I had called him over, after all.

He didn't look impatient. He looked calm and intense at the same time, which is the thing about him. How does a person look calm and intense at the same time? He is the only one I've ever seen do that.

"Um," I said.

He kept waiting.

"Do you, um, are you interested in . . ."

"In . . . ?" he prompted.

"Newspaper?"

"Newspaper?" he asked, just as I was thinking, *Huh? Newspaper? Did I just say "newspaper"?*

"Newspaper," I said, twirling my hair so hard it was possibly yanking bits of my brain too far to the left. "Are you, you know, going to be on, um, the newspaper? Staff? Or whatever?"

"I already am," he said. I already knew that, of course. What didn't I know about him? Please, I have his schedule memorized, I am so pathetic. "Why? Are you interested?"

"Yeah," I blurted. Sure. I was as interested in newspaper as I was in anything else lately that wasn't Kevin—meaning, NOT. "I am. Interested. In, in newspaper, I mean. Of course. Reporting!" I startled myself with the volume and enthusiasm of that last word.

"You should come, then," Kevin said, softly. "It's today after school. You're a good writer. You'd like it, I bet."

*A good writer,* he said. He had noticed me, in a positive way. I bobbled my books again but managed not to pitch them at Kevin's teeth. Any other person would be like, okay? Can we go into class before the bell rings? Or are you just going to stand there listing slightly to port all day? But Kevin just stood there in the doorway like he had no place else to go.

A good writer. What did that mean? Could that possibly really mean *I am in love with you, Charlie, and all I do is think about you all day long?*

Maybe. Unlikely, but maybe.

I lifted my eyes only, keeping my head down, and met his eyes. His head was bent, too, but he was looking at me. I didn't want to wreck the moment, but I did this thing, then, because I could feel myself smiling and the intensity of our little staring match was making me turn to wobbles: I leaned slightly closer to him.

I thought he would probably back away but he didn't. He tilted slightly closer to me, and I saw a little smile starting on his lips, too.

"Thanks," I whispered. I less-than-whispered. Almost no sound came out but this is how close we were standing: He heard me. I heard him breathe in.

I looked down, away, for fear I might lose my head and kiss him, stick my tongue back in his mouth again, as disgusting as that is. Disgusting and yet, kind of wonderful. I was close enough to him to feel the heat of him, the change in the air temperature, near his head.

*We're flirting,* I realized. I am flirting with him and I swear he is flirting right back with me.

I swallowed, squeezed my eyes shut, and forced myself to remember the actual reason I had called his name.

"One other thing," I said, my voice creaky. *She is my best friend,* I reminded myself again. But I admit this: I tilted my chin up, to give him a view of my neck, in case it actually was my best feature.

He raised his eyebrows and waited.

*Please say no,* I prayed. *Please say no.*

"Do you, um," I closed my eyes and finished fast: "Do you like Tess?"

He didn't say anything so I had to open my eyes and look at him. It is so unfair that his eyes are that color, like the lake in June.

"Do you?" I repeated, softer.

"Because I kissed her?" Kevin asked, his voice as quiet as mine.

"Because," I said, but I didn't know because what. Because she likes you, you doink. Then softer, "Do you?" *Say no! Say: I like you, Charlie.*

He didn't answer. I could feel my rib cage moving. I must have been panting. *Touch that strand of hair,* I silently begged. *I don't know what I'll tell Tess, who is my best friend in the world. But I want you—to like me, to choose me, to touch my hair, to kiss me—so much I can feel it, see it happening. . . .*

"Charlie," he said.

The bell rang. "What?"

I have to tell Tess I like him, too, I realized. I have to just tell her I didn't know I did, but I do. I like Kevin. And then there it would be and since we are best friends, always honest with each other, we would flip a coin for him or something.

Mrs. Roderick was standing above me and Kevin. "If you two are done flirting, it is time for science," she growled.

Flirting, me—flirting while I was fixing him up with my best friend. Mrs. Roderick had just confirmed it. My head was spinning. What the heck was I doing? It made no sense. Flirting. It felt delicious, dizzy. It felt—powerful. Nobody had ever mentioned that aspect of it to me. It was almost, well, indescribable.

"Almost done," Kevin said, and flashed Mrs. Roderick that grin of his. She batted her eyelashes at him. Twice. Mrs. Roderick is like a hundred and fifty years old. Kevin must be like the magnetic north of flirtation.

We headed toward our seats. Kevin sits behind me in bio. I was not about to try to steal him away from my best friend.

Not that I could, anyway.

Could I?

When we got to my seat, I whispered to Kevin, "So, do you?"

Kevin shrugged and whispered, "Sure," as he passed by me.

# eight

TESS WAS WAITING for me after class. I said, *He likes you*. She kissed me on the forehead and whispered *thanks*. Two hours later she asked him out, and he said *yes*, the jerk.

Fine. Just as well. Now I can move on with my life, concentrate on more important things. I was starting to annoy myself, honestly, all obsessed with a boy. I have always prided myself on not being a flirty girl. I have interests— well, not really, but I hope to develop some, and I probably have some talents that just haven't had a chance to bloom yet. But anyway, I am not like the Pop-Tarts. They are all so sweet and smiley and trendy, it is hard to tell which is which. I used to know some of them but it's increasingly difficult to tell them apart.

I am not a flirty girl.

I stayed for newspaper. Not because I wanted to be with Kevin, who has, in addition to dark blue eyes, a girlfriend—a girlfriend who is not only NOT me, but is my best friend, and besides, I remembered, I have a boyfriend, a very nice, smart, wonderful boyfriend, George. I went to newspaper because as someone mentioned, well, it was Kevin, I am a good writer and maybe I will become a journalist and write for the *New York Times* and win a Pulitzer Prize. And then certain people will realize how dumb they were not to fall in love with me when they had the chance.

Newspaper was somewhat interesting, in a way. The faculty advisor is Mr. McKinley. There's a rumor he used to be a priest. I could see immediately why he might not have been too successful in a comforting kind of role.

"Who are you?" he bellowed when I walked in.

I didn't know. My brain had melted in the heat of his voice.

He stepped closer and yelled again, "Who are you?"

Luckily it came to me: "Charlie."

"Charlie?" he yelled. "I have a brother named Charlie. You don't look anything like him."

"Thank you," I sputtered.

He laughed. Loud and long, like I'd genuinely cracked him up. He pounded me on the back with his meaty hand. "Good. I like you, Charlie. You here to be a reporter?"

I shrugged. I had no earthly idea what I was doing there.

"Good. Work the City News beat," Mr. McKinley

boomed. "We need a City News reporter. Right?"

I nodded, though of course I had no idea if they needed a City News reporter. He steered me past Kevin and some other kids sitting at the table, toward a girl at a computer in the back of the room.

"Penelope!" he shouted.

The girl looked up. She had crooked bangs and glasses and looked annoyed.

"Here's your City News staff. Her name is Charles. Put her to work!"

He turned to face the room and bellowed, "What is the most important element of a free society?"

"A free press," everybody answered in unison.

This club was obviously nuts. I considered a quick escape, but then Kevin smiled briefly at me before going back to what he was working on. I reminded myself that it did not matter to me at all if he smiled at me, and also that the most important something of a free society is a free press. I resolved not to even glance over at Kevin for at least the next five minutes. I checked the clock.

Penelope sighed. "There's hardly any city news. You can cover the Board of Ed. Okay?"

I had no idea what that meant. "Okay," I said.

"Do you know what that means?"

"Of course," I said. "But, well, sort of, no."

She rolled her eyes. "You go to the Board of Ed meetings. First Wednesday of every month, seven P.M. You take notes

47

and write them up for a story. Be accurate, be brief. Got it?"

"Sure."

"I'm applying early to Yale," she added. "Where do you want to go?"

"Home," I said.

"What?"

"Nothing," I said. "I'm not . . . I'm just a freshman."

"Gunning for editor in chief, huh?"

I shrugged. No, actually, I am only here because I have a crush on the boy I just fixed up with my best friend. I have no ambition in life beyond restraining myself from looking at him for another 4.5 minutes.

"Yeah, well, ed in chief is a lot better than City News editor on your applications, obviously." She sighed again. "I have other stuff, though, volunteer work, maybe a shot at valedictorian, and I fence. You don't fence, do you?"

"Like swords, or like picket?"

"What?"

"Nothing. No. I don't fence."

Sigh. "Get your stories in early and I'll rewrite them for you." Sigh. "I have five AP classes this year and the SATs coming up. I have to retake them, try for 2400. But don't try to scoop me—anything interesting comes up, it's mine. Got it?"

"Okay," I said. She had no idea how little she had to fear from me and my journalistic ambition.

I spent the rest of the afternoon just sitting at the table

doing my homework, trying not to attract either Penelope's or Mr. McKinley's attention. It worked. Nobody noticed me at all. Not even anybody with dark blue eyes. Not until later that night when he truly couldn't miss me.

# nine

"I THOUGHT YOU hated afterschool," Tess said. She's
been trying to get me to do drama or dance or chorus with
her forever.

"Yeah," I said. "Well."

"What did you stay for?"

I walked with her toward the bike rack. "Newspaper."

"Was Kevin there?"

"Um," I said. "I think so. Do you know some girl named
Penelope? She's a senior?"

Just then Kevin walked by. "Hey," he mumbled as he
passed us.

Neither of us answered; we just watched him board the
late bus.

We kind of smiled at each other, me and Tess. She

shrugged and said, "Knowing me, I give this thing with Kevin two weeks, maximum."

"Yeah," I said.

"Thanks."

"No! I meant . . ."

"I know, I know." She bent down to unlock her bike. "Do you really think he's a jerk?"

"Um . . ."

"You're probably right." Tess flung her long leg over the seat. "See you tomorrow. Sure you don't want me to ride you home?"

I shook my head. She rode off and I turned around. My walk home is the best part of my day. I tried not to think about Kevin, or Kevin and Tess, or kissing, but eventually gave up. I walked a long time, thinking about all of that.

I got home around five and did some random boring chatting online and also my homework, at the same time. Mom came in just as I was finishing. We stood in front of the refrigerator for a while together, and eventually came up with yogurt, bananas, string beans, and Froot Loops for dinner. Afterward we made a pot of decaf coffee and sat out on the deck with our mugs to look at the lake.

"Heck of a night," she said.

I nodded. The lake looked like a postcard image of itself, as if someone had painted a backdrop, and not a very realistic one either. The leaves were all gold and red and purple, and their reflections, upside down in the lake, were even nicer because of the blur. My mother had first seen the house at this time of year, and I can see why she made an offer on the spot, even if my father thought it was a money pit and the last straw.

Mom drained her cup. "Wanna go for ice cream?"

"Yeah," I said. Not much can get me off my butt on a nice night of lake looking, but ice cream is my weakness.

As we stomped into our shoes, Mom asked if anything interesting happened at school today. Well, let's see: I belly-flopped on the linoleum, flirted for the first time, fixed up my best friend with the boy I love, and began my career in journalism. "Nope," I said. "You?"

"Nope," she said, and grabbed her car keys off the hook.

We were not the only ones with the ice cream idea, apparently, so we ended up parking way down in the grocery store lot and walking up the hill. It was the last week of September but it felt like one of those end-of-summer evenings on the Cape, where my father and his cute new family live—one of those nights when there's a slight breeze and everybody wants to walk around in a hush and a cardigan, pleased with how it's all going.

Well, that was all dandy until I saw Kevin, already in line at Mad Alice's.

I felt myself slow down but then I gave myself a quick lecture: There is absolutely no reason for me to be freaked out about seeing a kid from my class at the ice cream place; it is a free country (with a free press!) and this is the best ice cream place around, with mush-ins and everything. And if the kid from my class just happens to be going out with my best friend, so what? And if that kid recently touched my tongue with his tongue—

*Stop it right there, Charlie. Do not think about his tongue or any other part of his body.*

"Hi," he said softly, almost to himself.

I managed not to do anything horribly humiliating like faint or, for instance, grab his head and start kissing him passionately right there on the sidewalk. Instead I went with saying, "Hi."

To get my eyes away from him I looked up at Mom, who hadn't said hello or introduced herself or anything. She was smiling at Kevin's father. He was smiling at her. I looked back and forth between them a couple of times before Mom broke eye contact with Kevin's father and looked down at the girl whose hand he was holding, and said, "You must be Samantha."

The girl nodded and held out her hand to shake Mom's. "Nice to meet you," she said.

Mom gave her a broad smile. "It's nice to meet you, too." My mother who prides herself on being cool and laid-back is such a sucker for manners. She shook Samantha's outstretched hand. "My name is Elizabeth. Elizabeth Reese."

Samantha turned to me and held out her hand. She had very few teeth, I noticed—one biggie in front surrounded by lots of space, which would make her, I guessed, about eight.

I shook her hand, feeling like a complete dork. I have never shaken hands with a kid before.

"Nice to meet you . . ."

"Charlie," I told her. "Hi. Um, nice to meet you, too."

We were at the door of Mad Alice's by then. Kevin's father held it open for us all. I noticed Kevin was giving his father a quizzical look like *what is wrong with you?* They'd been ahead of us in line, after all, and now he was, like, shepherding us in all as one group. But Kevin's father made a goofball face at Kevin and then smiled again at my mother, who blushed.

Blushed. I am not even kidding. Her cheeks turned bright red.

"What would you like, Charlie?" she asked.

"What?"

She pointed at the glass case in front of us. "Ice cream?"

I had lost my appetite. I mean, okay, Kevin's father is pretty hot for somebody old, for a dad. He has broad shoulders and sort of floppy brown hair and the same dark blue eyes as Kevin, except deeper set and in sort of a broader face. I could see how someone might argue this was a blushable thing, having this man smile at you so much and, I think, maybe even touch your back between your shoulder blades. I definitely think he did that. I had an obstructed view, it is true, as a journalist I have to admit that, but I do think that is exactly what he did: touched her on her back between her shoulder blades so lightly that he caused a chemical reaction that turned her cheeks bright red.

My *mother*.

"Charlie?"

"Um," I stalled. "Still thinking."

"Kevin?" his dad prompted.

"What? Um, I don't know yet. You go."

Samantha ordered lemon sorbet with butterscotch chips.

"Ew," Kevin and I both said at the same time.

My turn to blush. My family might be allergic to the Lazarus family.

I ordered fudge swirl with nonpareils mushed into it. Kevin had coffee with chocolate chips, which actually sounded even better than mine but no way was I copying. Mom got a mango sorbet cone, and Kevin's father said that sounded so good, he'd have the same.

As if Mom had invented the mango sorbet cone herself.

Mom paid for mine and hers, and Kevin's dad paid for his family's. That was a relief, at least. We all walked out together.

"Well," said Mom.

"Well," said Kevin's father.

They smiled at each other. Again. It was getting gross already.

"I've had enough," I said, and tossed the rest of my ice cream in the trash. Too bad if it is ridiculously expensive, and there is no reason to waste food. I was nearly puking on the sidewalk.

"Me, too," said Kevin, and tossed his in after mine.

We stood there for about an eternity, me, Kevin, and the garbage can. I tried to think of one thing in the world to say to him. I am normally pretty good at chatting.

"So," I said.

He didn't say anything so I looked up at him to see if he was busy doing something else. He looked up from the sidewalk at me at the same moment.

"Your sister seems . . ." I ran out of breath midsentence. That never happened to me before. It distracted me and then the pause was too huge and instead of finishing with, like, "nice," "smart," or "sweet," the three choices I'd been considering—I made a strange hiccuping/burping sound.

Kevin smiled. "You think?"

"Not that often," I answered.

"Was that a burp?"

"No!" I laughed. "No. It was a, just a, I don't know."

He nodded.

"A burp," I admitted falsely. "A small burp."

He laughed.

"She seems very smart."

"Yeah. She is."

He was still smiling. Maybe he likes burpy girls. I lifted my chin to show him, subtly, my good asset, in case he was reevaluating my worth in light of that newly discovered burping-noise aptitude.

"You okay?" he asked.

"Why?"

"Is something wrong with your head?"

"Why?"

"You just, never mind. I thought maybe you got a stiff neck at newspaper or something."

"No," I said, tipping my chin down. "I'm on City News staff," I added, to cover the fact that my head was bobbling, trying to get to a normal position. I could not seem to remember how it was supposed to balance on my neck.

"I'm on Features," Kevin said. "It's fun, when you get used to it."

"Yeah?" This was the longest conversation I'd ever had with him and I was making myself nauseous with my unsteady skull. I rested my hand on the garbage can for balance.

"Stick with it," he said quietly. "You'll see."

To avoid grabbing him and demanding to have another shot at kissing, I glanced over at Samantha and the adults. She was sitting on a bench and they were chatting near her. Mom's chin was tipped up. I squinted to get a look at her neck. It was long and graceful; I'd never noticed hers before either.

Do boys even like necks? Mr. Lazarus looked pretty happy over there.

Some scary-looking scruffy guys, who hang out on the Bridge at the front entrance to the high school, wandered slowly past me and Kevin, checking us out like they knew something about us. I hate when high school boys walk like that, leading with their scruffy-haired chins and coming too close to you, like they own everything. They act so entitled and scary, with their unbrushed hair and untucked shirts. I know that makes me sound horribly prudish and uncool, but the fact is, I am at heart prudish and uncool. I had a fleeting impulse to rush over and slip my hand into Mom's, for safety. Luckily I stopped myself.

Kevin just looked away, as if he were really fascinated by the stop sign down Hallowell Road. It occurred to me that the older boys might have been a little intimidating to him, too, which should have made me think he was a wimp but in fact made me like him that much more. There is nothing like silent vulnerability to make a girl crazy, as Tess has told me a million times. Another of her many theories I didn't understand, until very recently.

When the scruffy guys turned the corner, Kevin said, "So." It came out kind of high and squeaky. He repeated, "So," in a very, overly, deep voice. I smiled and at that exact moment, Mom and Kevin's father and sister came over.

"Should we go?" Mom asked.

I nodded.

"Nice to meet you," Samantha said, and started another round of hand-shaking.

"I'm a kid," I told her.

"I know," she said.

"So we should just, like, stand here awkwardly and say bye, and then, like, wait impatiently for the adults to finish shaking hands."

My mother found this hilarious, apparently, because she laughed a really loud snorting laugh, and Kevin's father cracked up, too.

"Okay," Samantha said. "Bye." She arranged her legs into an awkward stance and stood there watching the adults with an impatient expression souring her face.

"Much better," I said.

"Thank you," she said, and smiled a smile so crushingly similar to Kevin's I had to look at him to compare. He wasn't smiling, though. He may have kind of waved, or else maybe there was a mosquito near his head.

Neither Mom nor I said anything in the car, and when we got home I went right upstairs. I heard Mom out on the deck, probably reading, drinking a glass of wine. She came up a while later. I was lying on my bed.

She flipped off my light and said good night.

"Mom," I said.

She leaned against my door frame and waited. She looked really pretty, with the hall light behind her and her high cheekbones really noticeable.

"Did you know they were going to be there tonight?"

She took a deep breath in, seeming to consider her answer, which basically answered it for me. I closed my eyes.

"Yeah," she said, but when I opened my eyes, she was gone.

# ten

BREAKFAST WAS A little awkward, since Mom and I couldn't quite look at each other or talk beyond, "Oh, did you want the juice? Sorry." All very polite. I was early to the bus stop for once.

At school Kevin and I avoided each other completely. Overall, though, this whatever-it-was, stress, turned out to be quite a boost for my schoolwork—I threw myself into concentrating in class. I copied over my notes at night and really studied, and got 100s on both quizzes (math and bio).

I also swam thirty-six laps (there and back counts as one, by the way), which is a mile, every day after school. I even hurried through the woods. The woods make me think. Swimming makes me stop thinking.

Wednesday night I went to the Board of Ed meeting.

I took notes the whole time. I had no idea what they were talking about and I have to admit that some of my notes were doodles of the board members.

Friday, Penelope stopped me in the hall. "Where's your story?"

"Not done yet," I said.

She looked shocked. "You better have it to me by fourth period. It has to be in final form by eighth!" She stormed away, muttering under her breath.

I spent a big chunk of my lunch period writing the thing, while eavesdropping on Tess and Jen and Darlene's gossiping—well, and sometimes adding my opinion. Occasionally. They were choosing new rings for all our cell phones, which was considerably more compelling as a subject than my boring article. It was just hard to care too much about a Board of Ed meeting. I didn't even really get what was going on there, and couldn't imagine any other student at our school caring one bit either. I was only doing it because I am an idiot and have this psychotic need to sit in a room with my best friend's boyfriend one afternoon a week. I should just quit, but, as someone said one time, I am a good writer. And as someone else said, I am in need of a hobby. And see? I am a natural at quoting people—so maybe I will get used to it and have fun, as the first someone promised.

I get distracted even inside my own head.

I did what I could with truly anesthetizing material, then tore it out of my spiral and tracked down Penelope before fifth.

"This is it?" she asked, holding the three ragged pages as if she could catch a disease from them.

I shrugged. "Yeah."

Penelope sighed. "It's supposed to be a fifty-word nugget, max."

"Fifty nuggets?"

"Fifty words."

"Oh, are you talking about the article?"

"What did you think I was talking about?"

"A Happy Meal."

"A what?"

"You said something about how many nuggets . . ."

"That's a news term. Fifty-word nugget, max."

"Not Max," I said. "Charlie."

"I know your name." She scrunched her face at me. "Are you kidding, or an idiot?"

"Do I have to choose?"

The bell rang before we could continue this enlightening conversation, so I bolted. Good thing Kevin isn't on the football team; I'd get my butt kicked literally then.

Friday night Tess came over for a sleepover. I had already showered after swimming and done all my homework for Monday before she showed up, sweaty from her bike ride. She takes the long way and zooms. "Want to swim?" she asked, breathless and sweaty when she came in. "I brought my suit."

I said okay, despite the wobbly feeling in my legs. I

grabbed my only clean suit and we hiked up to the club-house.

I signed in again and Chris, who is the cutest door guy, cocked his head to say Tess could just go ahead without being signed in and giving us a guest fee to pay on our bill.

"Thanks," she said to him, lowering her eyelids slowly.

He winked at her.

He is probably, like, twenty. She flashed him a smile and we ran into the women's locker room.

I opened my mouth wide at her.

She shrugged. "He's cute."

"Yeah," I said. I shook my head and we found a locker that was empty. Guys who are possibly past being teenagers wink at Tess? "Wow," I said. "Has that happened to you before?"

"What?" Tess asked, and pulled off her shirt. She has no body-shyness at all, never has, as long as I've known her. She stepped out of her shorts and underpants, then yanked off her sports-bra and began getting into her bathing suit. "You gonna watch?" she asked.

I sat down on the bench and took off my own shirt. My arms were heavy from earlier.

"I was thinking," she started.

"Always dangerous," I said.

"Very true." She was already shoving her hair into her bathing cap. "What if I decided to train for a triathlon?"

"A what?" My bathing suit was a little pilly on the butt.

My good one was already wet from before, and my medium ones were in the hamper.

"Triathlon. You have to run, swim, and bike." She pulled her goggles over her eyes. She looked like a bug.

I smiled. "You'd win," I said.

"You're the best," she said. "Ready?"

I followed her to the pool and we swam for a while. I was surprised I could do it, honestly. Maybe my muscles are building up. Maybe I could do a triathlon, too, if I could get interested in biking and running. Or maybe I could just be an Olympic swimmer. If the whole journalism thing doesn't pan out, I could dedicate myself completely to swimming and not have time to waste thinking about which boy is cute, or who he likes, or what the hell is going on with my mother and his father. That might be a good goal.

"I need a goal," I told Tess, on the way to the locker room.

"Goals are for soccer," she said.

We showered, dried off, got dressed in our already worn clothes and hiked back to my house. Mom was digging the big wooden bowl out of the cabinet when we walked into the kitchen.

"Hi, Elizabeth," Tess called.

"Hey, Tess!" My mother always sounds so happy when she talks to Tess. Tess is *my* friend, I sometimes think of reminding her. She gave us each a kiss on our damp heads. "I'm making refrigerator salad."

Tess heaved herself up to sit on the counter and grabbed

a string bean out of the bag beside her. "My favorite," she said. In Tess's family, like in my father's, there is old-fashioned dinner every night: "three things on a plate," we call it—a meat, a vegetable, a starch. Mom and I go for a more laissez-faire approach, which means, if my French is right (ouch, probably not) "let it be," or possibly "they let do," though, as has been proven, French is not my forte. Anyway, the height of our style is refrigerator salad, which means (and this I do know) any bits and pieces we have leftover in the fridge, tossed in a bowl, with lemon squeezed on top and a dash of best-quality olive oil.

"Taste this," Mom insisted, pouring a drop of the olive oil onto some bread she must have picked up on her way home.

Tess opened her mouth and Mom put the bread in. "Yum," murmured Tess.

"There is nothing like excellent olive oil," Mom said, giving me a taste, too. How generous, her own daughter.

It was good. "Mmm," I admitted.

I got out three stem glasses, and Tess took down three of the big serving bowls we use for our refrigerator salads.

"Oh," said Mom, turning around. "Just two, tonight."

"Is one of us leaving?" I asked, hoping it wasn't me.

"I'm, um," Mom said, "Going out. Tonight."

"On a date?" Tess asked.

I like it that my friends are friends with my mother, but honestly.

"Out with some colleagues."

My mother doesn't go on dates. She goes to meetings. Occasionally a seminar.

"Who's the lucky guy?" Tess bit her lower lip, psyched.

I gripped the counter for support.

Mom grinned. "Tess! About a third of the American history department."

"Ooo," said Tess. "A woman of mystery."

"History, not mystery." Mom hit Tess with some limp celery. "So, you girls have fun. I have to get ready."

We watched her go.

Tess kicked me.

"Ow," I said, and not just from the kick.

"She has a boyfriend?"

I rolled my eyes. "It's not a date."

"Oh, come on," Tess said. "It is so a date!"

"If it is, it is," I said wearily. Tess is great, but sometimes she pushes. It was not a date, obviously. It was a meeting. It was colleagues. They would probably be discussing the Reconstruction period, as usual. She had those people over sometimes.

"Does she go on a lot of dates?"

"How many is a lot?"

"I don't know," Tess said.

"Such a vague term."

"Every week?"

"How about never? Is never a lot? Zero—I think that would fall below the 'a lot' threshold. It is not a date, Tess." I blew air fast out of my lips, the way Darlene does sometimes when she's being dismissive. On me it sounded a bit like a lawn mower.

"Okay," Tess said, looking slightly wounded.

"It's not."

"Sorry."

"It's just—you shouldn't tease her like that. She's getting old, you know, she's over forty, and she doesn't date, and I think she doesn't mind, but she doesn't need to feel, you know, judged. By my friends, of all people."

"Ouch," Tess said. "I wasn't trying to—sorry. Okay?"

"I just, I try to stay out of her personal life," I said, which wasn't exactly a lie. Up until this week she didn't really have a personal life, or if she did I certainly didn't know about it. And it was completely possible that she still had no personal life.

"Well," Tess said, eating another string bean. "Anyway."

"Yeah," I said.

Tess and I ate our salads together sitting at the breakfast bar. They were good. There was corn, which always zests it up. Mom came down and gave us another round of kisses. She was wearing her funky red clogs, a T-shirt, her yellow denim jacket, and jeans, all normal—plus lip gloss and mascara. Not normal. She looked beautiful.

"Have fun," Tess said.

"You, too," Mom said, grabbing her keys from the hook. "I won't be late. Be good, and call me on my cell if you need me."

*I need you now*, I randomly thought. "Bye," I said, and watched her walk out the door.

"Where do you think she's going?" Tess asked. "With her colleagues."

"Shut up," I said.

"We should check and see if she still has that lip gloss on when she gets home," Tess whispered. "That's how my mom busted my sister Lena for kissing—swollen lips, no more gloss."

Before I could puke, the phone rang.

# eleven

"HELLO?"

It was Kevin's voice, but I was not about to make the same mistake twice. "Hello," I said, all neutral, though my hand was shaking so much the phone clanked against my head.

"It's Kevin," the voice said.

"Who is it?" Tess whispered.

I gave her the "sh" sign and said, "Hi."

"Did, um," he said. "Is your . . . Did we get any homework in French for over the weekend?"

"No," I said. How awkward that he would say the word *French* to me, given our history. I leaned against the wall for support.

"Who is it?" Tess demanded.

I stuck my finger in my exposed ear. "We never do on Fridays."

"Oh, yeah," he said. "I forgot. I was looking in my assignment pad and I didn't . . . um . . . that's a lie, by the way. You knew that, right?"

I smiled. I closed my eyes. I wanted to make this last. "Yeah." *Kevin.*

"Who?" Tess tried to grab the phone.

I put my hand over the talkie part and whispered, "It's Kevin. I bet he's looking for you. *Sh.*"

Tess grinned wickedly at me and sat back down. She loves a scheme.

"That obvious?" Kevin asked.

"Yeah," I said into the phone. "So why are you really calling?" I grinned back at Tess. Sometimes you have to feel sorry for boys. They do not know what they're up against. I jutted my hips to the side. I was in this thing, this some-thing, this teasing of a boy, with Tess. I was powerful and beyond him, up to something. We had done this to boys before, for years. At least it was familiar territory.

"Um, because," said Kevin. "Is, I was wondering . . ."

I sank down, against the wall, to the floor. "Yeah?"

I heard him breathing. "Is your . . ."

I closed my eyes.

"What did he say?" Tess whispered. I looked up at her, her chin cupped in her hand, all excited and happy. "What does he want?"

I tried to smile back, and into the phone I said, "Did you call to talk to Tess?" My voice had lost some of its jauntiness, but I was trying.

Tess apparently failed to notice. She opened her mouth wide, still having fun, and flung her shoe at me. It just missed my head and left a mark on the wall.

"No," said Kevin. "Why?"

I closed my eyes. The smile I was faking was wearing me out. "Well, you tracked her down."

"Oh," said Kevin.

"You want to talk to her?"

"Um," he said, and I handed the phone up to Tess. I listened, sort of, with my head between my knees and my arms wrapped around them. Tess was laughing at something Kevin said. I love her wicked laugh. I didn't lift my head again until she said bye and hung up.

"That was weird," she said as we washed the dishes. "Want to see what's on TV?"

I nodded and followed her into the living room. We flopped together onto the couch and watched TV, head to toe. With my feet burrowed under her, I thought about Tess's boyfriend and wondered why he had called me. Any time I glanced at Tess I had to think, she has no idea what a bad friend I am, keeping secrets from her, flirting with her boyfriend. I decided right then and there to put a stop to it: no more flirting, no more liking him. If he wants to break up with Tess and then, many weeks later, ask me out, I'll consider it. The double life is too horrible and stressful for me. *Good-bye, Kevin,* I thought. *This is the last hour I will ever spend imagining kissing you again.*

The TV blared, Tess dozed, I imagined. We barely moved until Mom came home.

# twelve

MOM WAS ALL fake-surprised to find us awake on the couch and, I noticed sadly, lip-gloss-free. She hustled us upstairs to bed. While we were brushing our teeth, Tess whispered, "She sure has F.K.G., huh?"

"Who has what?" I asked, thinking she was talking about fried chicken.

"Your mom," Tess said. "F.K.G.—Freshly Kissed Glow."

"Please don't make me vomit in front of you," I said, and sat on the rim of the bathtub. I had a mouthful of toothpaste but visions of my mother kissing Kevin's father made me too woozy to stand, so I had to spit into the tub.

Tess rinsed her mouth the standard way.

"Charlie!" Tess said. "Are you okay?"

"Yeah," I answered. "Yeah, I'm fine. I am. I just sometimes

like to spit my toothpaste in the tub. For fun! And, but, with my mom? The thing is, she just is not great at, she doesn't wear lip gloss, you know, enough to know you have to reapply it after you drink a cup of . . ."

"Oh, Charlie." She sat down beside me on the rim, with her arm around me. I rested my head on her shoulder. "You know what we're gonna do?"

I could so not handle a Tess scheme right then, especially if it related to my mother's love life or, even worse, kissing life. "Tess . . ."

"What we're going to do," interrupted Tess, "is we are not going to talk about it. Discussing other people's F.K.G. is gross, especially grown-ups', and especially especially parents'. Right?"

"Right." I wiped my nose on my sweatshirt sleeve exactly the way that drives my father nuts—up, so it gives me a crease in my nose. But right then I just didn't care.

"I mean, I couldn't discuss my parents getting F.K.G. They never have it," Tess said. "I don't think they've kissed since I was a baby. Their mouths are too busy screaming at us."

"My mother was not on a date."

"Okay," Tess said.

"She was at a meeting."

"I know."

"So let's not discuss what doesn't even exist," I said.

"Exactly." Tess stood up. "Do you have a headband?"

I shook my head.

"Don't worry," Tess said.

If only my main worry was my lack of a headband.

Tess pulled off her underwear from under her huge nightshirt, yanked the band of it down around her ears, and tucked in her hair. She even looked pretty like that. Odd, for sure, but still pretty. She always does. I couldn't help staring.

"What?" She turned and looked at me, all matter-of-fact. "Otherwise my hair will get wet when I wash my face. What do you do?"

*What do I do?* It was too big a question. What I don't do is stand in my bathroom with underwear on my head, two tufts of hair sprouting up from the leg holes, and water dripping off my face. Just when I thought nothing could seem funny to me, though, Tess does something like this. I shrugged.

"Let's talk about *you* kissing instead," she said, lathering up her face with her special face stuff from Filene's.

"Me?"

"When are you going to put poor George out of his misery and kiss him?"

I groaned and splashed some water on my own face.

"Why are you so scared to kiss? It's nice. You'll like it, I think."

I grabbed a towel.

"Aren't you going to at least exfoliate?" she asked.

"That's what it always comes down to in life, isn't it? Kiss e." I shook my head. "I'm going to bed."

ust have to get your first kiss behind you, Charlie.

'll see what I mean."

she got to my room (underpants mercifully back where they belong, I had to assume, or at least off her head) we talked for a while about why Kevin had called her at my house and if that was romantic or creepy. I said I thought it was just medium. I think she was hoping I'd vote for romantic. She has not been in love since last Memorial Day weekend, with Luke Sorenson, and that was really short-lived, didn't even last through that Monday. Elliot Blumenfeld was her first love, last fall. Then in January it was Widge Wainwright, which I didn't get at all; he is so beige. She had fallen out of love with him by February second but held out until the fourteenth, then broke up with him when he didn't even give her a card, never mind candy, for Valentine's Day.

While she was talking, I was thinking that I really should tell her I already had gotten my first kiss behind me, and that it changed nothing, really. But then she'd be so mad at me for not telling her earlier, maybe she'd never forgive me. And the last thing I needed right then was to lose my best friend. I had crossed a line, at some point, by not telling her already. *It never happened,* I reminded myself; if Kevin ever says it did, I can just say "you wish" or something mature like that.

"I think he might be the one," Tess was saying.

"Who's the one? The one what?"

"Kevin," she said. "The real one for me, the one I'm

destined to be with forever, or at least through high school."

"Really?"

"The one I'll tell my kids about someday. There's real tragedy in his eyes, you know what I mean?" she asked.

"Yeah," I said, staring at the ceiling from down on the air mattress. "Sort of. You mean how he looks calm and intense at the same time?"

She lifted her head and rested it on her hand, her elbow bobbing on the mattress. "Exactly! I can't believe you just said that. Do you think it's because his mom ran away from home to be a fighter pilot?"

"Is that really true?" I knew the rumor, of course; everybody did. I couldn't help suspecting it was probably both simpler and more complicated—maybe Kevin's parents, like my own, had at some point just stopped loving each other.

"Yes, it's totally true," Tess said. "She's in the Middle East, I heard—Jennifer's father is friends with Kevin's father, and Jennifer told me, like, last week. Kevin's mom is in, um, whatever—one of those countries that starts with an I, totally flying jets. Isn't that cool, in a way? I mean, sucks for the kids, but still. If it's her passion, what she dreamed of doing all her life, you know? Like when other little girls were pretending to be Cinderella, she was totally, like, bombing enemy aircraft in her backyard. Right? I have the whole story worked out in my head."

"So I see," I said. Tess always makes up a whole story for everything. It's one of the best things about a sleepover with her. She has life stories worked out for all the cafeteria ladies, old men in the mall, everybody. "So then what happened?" I asked. "Why did she get married and have kids?"

"Oh, isn't that so obvious and sad?" Tess sat up, psyched. "She felt all this pressure to conform, maybe from her mother or friends or an older sister—yes, I think it was an older sister, who was more traditional and already happily married—and then of course she met Kevin's father. I mean, he is hot, right?"

My stomach actually made a noise.

"Your guts know it," Tess said, pointing. "He's old and he's still a hottie, so you can imagine how hot he was when he was young. So she met him and they fell in love and you know she was all off balance, falling in love with someone like that. So she tried to be ordinary, make her parents proud and happy like her sister had, tried to forget flying and her own career and all and maybe he insisted on it, Kevin's father—he wanted her to stay home and make three-things-on-a-plate dinners and go to PTA meetings. So she tried to be that person but all her dreams, when she fell into her insomniac sleep at night, were fighter pilot dreams and eventually she just couldn't fake it anymore; she just couldn't be someone she wasn't, even for the man she loved. Did you know Kevin has a little sister? Amanda, I think."

"Samantha," I said accidentally. I was so caught up in the story of this woman's life, I wanted to hear how it turned out.

"Right. Samantha. The mom supposedly left when the little girl was, like, two. Talk about messing a kid up. But maybe being abandoned by his mother is kind of what makes Kevin so passionate, you know?"

"Tess!"

"What?"

"She didn't abandon . . . That didn't even . . . You're making it all up."

"So?"

"So you can't know what really happened between them. Besides, that is such a mean way to put it. Abandoned?"

"Okay, I wasn't auditioning to be his therapist. He's not even here. I was complimenting him anyway, Miss Protector of the Kevin."

I hit her with my pillow.

Tess flipped over onto her stomach and stuffed my pillow under her arms. "Here's the thing. I wish you'd kissed him, too."

I froze. *What?* "You do?"

"So you'd know what I mean. Because he does this thing, when he kisses, or at least when he kissed me at your party."

"What?"

"Promise you won't mock me," she said.

"I won't," I promised. "I swear. What did he do?"

"He kind of, like, almost groaned a little when he kissed me."

His secret hum-sigh. No. That was only for me. I tried

79

to swallow, unable to speak.

"You know what I mean?" Tess asked. "It's hard to explain." She imitated it, the sound Kevin made when he kissed me. He made it with her, too, I guess. So either he makes that private sound of longing with every girl he kisses or every boy does that. It was hard not to be overwhelmed with disappointment.

"Do you think that's weird? Or good?"

"I don't know," I admitted.

"Oh, Charlie, you really have to start kissing so we can discuss this better."

I closed my eyes.

"At Kevin's party." Tess sat up and leaned toward me. "Kiss George next week at Kevin's party."

"Tess . . ."

"Come on," Tess prodded. "I'll kiss Kevin and you kiss George. Let's make a pact."

"I don't know," I said. "I think I'm just not that into kissing, maybe."

"You are crazy," Tess said, grabbing me by the shoulders. Her face was maybe three millimeters from mine. "Listen to me. Kissing is the best thing ever invented."

She had a look of total seriousness on her face. I wasn't sure what I was supposed to do. I stayed very still.

She clonked her forehead against mine and cracked a smile. "With the possible exception of gummy bears," she added.

She scrunched her nose, then flipped over and snuggled down into her pillow. "So it's a pact then. We kiss them on Halloween. No backing out."

She closed her eyes. In a minute I heard her breathing slow into sleep. I stared at the ceiling and thought about her boyfriend again, despite my recent and sacred personal vow not to.

# thirteen

TESS WANTED ME to go as half a banana and she'd be the other half, so together we'd be, obviously, a banana—split. But I'd already had another idea so she did the banana thing with Jennifer. I went as a lawn: green turtleneck, green cords, and a pink flamingo Beanie Baby pinned to my shoulder. We loved ourselves, how witty we were. Darlene wanted to come over before the party, too, so I said sure, despite dreading that she'd be dressed, as usual, as a prostitute. But no, she pulled through. She had on a whole roll of tinfoil, poufed out over her miniskirt, and a beret with a long white paper coming out the top that said "La Hershey La Hershey" on it.

"I give up," I said.

"I'm a French kiss!"

Even Jennifer had to admit that was pretty good.

My mom came down in the witch's hat that she wears every Halloween, and a new black sweater with her black jeans and boots.

"Is that new?" I asked.

"Yes," Mom said, running her hand over her stomach. "Thanks for noticing."

I hadn't intended it as a compliment, though the sweater did make her look good. Curvy. My father's wife, Suzie, wears blouses and floral prints that hang nowhere near her body. I used to like it that my mom was less inhibited than Suzie.

"Can we just go?" I asked.

Tess smirked at me. "Getting psyched, huh?"

I ignored that. She had mentioned our kissing pact a couple of times and though I tried to point out that I hadn't officially agreed, Tess was, like, have your lawyer call me, you're not getting out of the pact, you wimp, so you'd better practice puckering.

We piled into the car. I sat in front. Mom put on Bruce Springsteen, who was moaning "If you love me tonight I promise I'll love you forever." More pacts. I closed my eyes.

"Mom?"

She said nothing but turned down the music a bit.

"You're not staying, are you? At the party?"

"I thought I might," she answered. "It's a family party, adults as well as kids. That's what I heard. All ages welcome."

Tess and Darlene groaned in the backseat.

"No, Mom, it's not."

"But . . ."

"Mom, we're in ninth grade!"

"Yes, Charlotte, I am aware of that, but . . ."

"Forget it." I kept my eyes closed and concentrated on the sound of the saxophone. I played saxophone in middle school and it never sounded remotely like that.

"Is that okay?" my mother asked me quietly. "If I stay?"

No. Obviously, not.

But I said nothing. What more could I say? She obviously didn't care when I said it was NOT a party for her, it was for me, us, the kids.

I didn't open my eyes until she stopped the car and put it into park. My friends were already spilling out the back doors.

"Your costume is great," Mom whispered.

"Thanks," I grumbled.

"Do I look okay?" she asked.

I opened my door and turned away from her.

"I mean I know it's hackneyed," she said. "But I was thinking that was kind of the fun of it, unless people don't get it and think it's just unimaginative . . ."

"Which people?" I got out and shut the door, not really wanting to hear her answer.

I caught up to my friends and went up the walk to the back door. Tess said, "You okay?"

I shrugged.

"My mother would never want to be at a party with me," Darlene said.

"Lucky," I said.

"You think?" Darlene asked.

"Let's just go in," Jennifer suggested, so we did. I don't think they really wanted to show up at the party with my mom either, so we let the door close behind us as Mom was heading up the walk. *Too bad if that's rude,* I decided.

The party was in the room I think was supposed to be the dining room, except that instead of a dining table there was a pool table. I spotted George as soon as I got there. Well, he was pretty hard to miss. George is not what you'd call a skinny guy, though he is definitely not fat; he told me once that his mother said he has big bones. He was wearing a white turtleneck that was all bulged out by a pillow or two underneath, and a furry panda bear hat tied onto his head. He gave me a big smile and headed toward me.

"It's gonna be hard to kiss him past all that," Tess whispered. "You'll have to make him sit down."

"Shut up," I said, scanning the room, subtly I hoped, for Kevin. I located him beside the drinks table, dressed as a vampire. It was just black pants, white button-down shirt, red bow tie, his hair slicked back with gel, and some makeup—whitened skin, black around his eyes, red on his mouth. In a sane state of mind I would have dismissed that get-up as being as hackneyed as my mother's witch suit, but my hormones had apparently knocked me semiconscious: He looked so hot my mouth dropped open.

"Hey," George said.

He startled me. I'd forgotten him again.

"What?" I sounded defensive, even to myself, and beside me Jennifer jumped at the shrillness of my voice.

"Good article," George said.

"Right."

"It was."

"I couldn't even find it," I said truthfully. I had had to read through the entire paper twice, once at school and later at home, before I could find my piece. It had been that kind of week.

"Come on," George said. "It was there."

"It was a tiny block, with no byline." I had intended to sound confident and shrugging so the poutiness of my own voice surprised me.

George touched my shoulder. "Well . . ."

"And it had almost no information—only the date, time, and location of the board meeting." Penelope had cut all my musings and filler. It was basically more of a notice than an article. "How did you even know it was mine?"

"You told me you were covering it," he said. "So I looked."

"Nice party," I commented to change the subject.

"Yeah, I guess. You look, um, nice. Good. As always. But, um, what are you dressed as?"

"A lawn."

"A lawn?"

"Yeah. Get it?"

"With a Beanie Baby left out on it?"

"A flamingo. Get it? Like, you know, when people put plastic flamingos on their lawns?"

"Who does?"

"Some people," I said, trying to look past him at Kevin, who wasn't budging from his spot across the room.

"Really? Plastic flamingos? On their lawns? Why would people do that?"

"I don't know, George. What are you supposed to be?"

He tilted his head and tried to make eye contact with me. "A panda."

"Oh," I said, hating myself for being such a bitch. "Good one."

He stood there for another second or two, then said, "Thanks." When I still wouldn't look at him, he looked away, then asked, "You see the weather report today?"

"The what?" I asked. Then remembering having been all freaked out on the phone with him about the weather report and its lack of long-term significance, I said, "No." I'd figured he wasn't even listening that day. I wasn't really talking about the weather report then, anyway. It was just a metaphor, as my English teacher, Ms. Lendzion, would say, for how bad it was that Kevin liked me for such a short time I hardly got to enjoy it. Not that I was about to explain that to George, my boyfriend. Boys don't get metaphors.

"Oh," he said, and kept standing there, with his face turned away.

Then I felt guilty for acting that rude, so I reluctantly asked, "Why did you want to know about the weather?"

"I saw it," George said. "The weather report."

"Yeah?" I said, thinking nastily, *And your point is?*

"Yeah," he said. "Right up there on the top corner of the newspaper."

I so did not want to talk about the weather. "Oh," I said. "Is there anything we should know about tomorrow's weather, then? Because I guess it's too late for today."

"Nope," he said. "Nothing at all. Just . . ." But he didn't say anything else and after a minute he walked away.

"Ouch," Jennifer whispered.

I let out my breath. "I hate parties," I whispered.

"Let's get drinks," Tess whispered to me.

She grabbed my belt loop but I hung back.

"Lighten up, drama queen," she whispered. "Come on."

"I'll go," Darlene said.

"Okay." Tess shot me a look and crossed the room with her. Jennifer and I leaned our backs against the wall for a few minutes, watching the girls who had the guts to talk to the boys. I couldn't hear what Tess was saying or see her face, so I just stared at Kevin's, and watched a slow, sexy smile spread across his mouth to reveal plastic white fang teeth.

A little sound escaped from somewhere in my throat.

I watched him looking at Tess. It was all I could do to stay upright.

"Yeah," Jennifer said. "Want to find the bathroom?"

I nodded and pushed off from the wall. But what I should've known by then, after what happened at my own party, was that you never know what you might find around a corner at a party.

# fourteen

WE WANDERED AROUND for a few minutes, but there wasn't an obvious bathroom. Kevin's house is all on one level, very modern-looking. We were about to head down a hallway when Kevin's best friend, Brad, rounded the corner. He is a nut. He was dressed as a pregnant cheerleader. "Where do you think you're going?" he demanded.

"Where's the bathroom?" Jennifer asked him.

"Next to the front door," he said. "Have fun!"

"Shut up," Jennifer said. She started chewing her cuticles. It occurred to me that even Jen might have dramas of her own going on. We headed toward the front door.

"Hey," I said to her, leaning close. "Do you like . . ."

"No," she answered quickly. I decided not to push it.

Jennifer knocked on the slim door beside the massive

double front door. A voice from inside said, "One sec," sounding surprised and embarrassed.

"Was that Kevin?" I whispered.

Jennifer nodded.

We took a few steps away, not wanting to embarrass him when he came out, not wanting him to think we were listening. I remember in kindergarten there was a bathroom in our classroom, and it was so incredibly hard to do what you desperately needed to do because you knew there were other kids right outside the door hearing you.

But when the door opened, it was not Kevin who emerged. It was Kevin's dad.

*AND:* my mother.

With no lip gloss, only F.K.G.

And behind them was not the bathroom, I couldn't help noticing. It was a coat closet.

Nobody said anything. What was there to say? What the hell were you two doing in the coat closet? That is not exactly a question you want to be asking your mother.

"What the hell were you two doing in the coat closet?" I asked.

"Charlie," said Mom, properly identifying the asker.

"We, um, hanging . . . coats," said Kevin's father. "Up."

"I . . ." I didn't know what else to say. I felt Jennifer tugging my sleeve.

"Did you need to, um, hang a coat?" Kevin's dad asked. "Up?" His face was red and I noticed he was wearing a tux and the bow tie was crooked. What was he dressed as, a fancy man? How creative, a fancy man. A coat check man? Or just a checking-out-my-mother-in-the-coat-closet man? Oh, what a cool costume.

"Sorry," Jennifer said, and yanked me away, toward the kitchen. "Come on," she said to me. "Let's take a walk."

Jennifer and I walked around the block without talking, and then around again. As the house came into sight, she asked, "How you doing?"

"Don't tell anybody," I said.

"I won't."

"I know," I said. I looked at her and took a deep breath. I prayed Jennifer wouldn't give me any bull like it's okay, your mom is entitled, they are both single consenting adults and doesn't she deserve to be happy. I had all that going on in my head, doing battle with the other side that was screaming *but she is my mother!*

Then another thought hit me. "Aren't your parents friends with Kevin's parents?"

"Yeah," Jennifer said.

I covered my face with my hands. "Great."

"Some things are private," Jennifer said. "Even from parents."

I nodded. "Thanks. You're a good friend."

"I know," said Jennifer. She put her arm lightly around my shoulder and we went back inside.

"I can't believe his mother is in Iraq," I said.

"Whose mother?"

"Kevin's. Flying fighter jets," I whispered. "In Iraq. Right? Or Iran, maybe?"

"Idaho," Jennifer said. "She's in Idaho. I don't think she flies anything. Maybe a kite occasionally. She's the most aggressively mellow person ever; she, like, goes on marches for peace. A fighter pilot? That is a really funny image. My parents would love that. Why would you think she was a fighter pilot?"

"Tess said you told her . . ."

Jennifer cocked her head and raised her eyebrows. "Tess says a lot of things."

"Then why do Kevin and Samantha live with their father?"

Jennifer shrugged. "My parents said that's the arrangement that everybody wanted. But who really knows?"

By then we'd gotten back to the party room. I half-expected Tess to be making out with Kevin, but luckily I was spared that one horror. Darlene and Tess were dancing over by the stereo, talking to Brad, who was choosing music. Kevin was shooting pool with some of the other guys. George looked up as I came in. His flash of a smile changed to a perplexed look, and he mouthed, "You okay?"

I nodded and looked away. I knew I was completely incapable of conversation right then, especially about if I was okay and why not. The last thing I wanted ever, but particularly right then, was a scene. I just wanted to have fun, enjoy the party, not deal, forget.

But no.

Kevin's dad and my mom tromped into the room, holding a stack of pizza boxes. They were smiling as if they were the parents of the house, and we were a winning Little League team. "Who's hungry?" Kevin's dad asked. He put his two boxes down, and my mother put her two beside his.

"Hot!" she said, and I almost could have killed her on the spot.

I may have actually flown across the room. I don't remember walking, certainly, and there was a pool table between us; anyway, there I was, and I grabbed her arm, hard. "Can I talk to you?"

"Sure," she said. "Ow."

I stormed out of the room and she followed me. I think probably everybody was watching us but at that point I didn't even care. Or not that much. Well, I cared but I added that humiliation to all the other stuff I was blaming her for in my head.

"What is wrong with you?" I calmly asked her in the hall. Well, calmly might be an exaggeration. I kind of yelled. Kind of might be an exaggeration, too. Okay, I was shrieking.

"Charlie," she said, incredulous.

"Right again," I said.

"What?"

"Why are you ruining my life?" I asked, even louder, if that's possible.

"Charlotte Reese Collins," she said. "Control yourself."

Two girls dressed as goths went by. Mom and I both smiled and nodded as they passed, then turned furious faces back to each other.

"Control myself?" I asked. "Look who's talking!"

I thought she was going to slap me, I really did. Her hand went up toward my face. She'd never slapped me before and she believes it's unforgivable to strike a child, but in fact I am probably not a child anymore so I wasn't sure if all bets were off on that rule, and besides, I kind of deserved it. Still, I was a tiny bit proud. It usually takes me until the next day to think of a good comeback.

Instead of slapping me, though, she grabbed my shoulder and steered me, hard, toward the kitchen. There were like six or eight people crowded around the refrigerator, grabbing stuff. We tried the living room but it was wide-open and white, looking like *don't come in.*

We stopped there in the hall and faced each other. We took deep breaths. The spot was not ideal but the battle had to take place somewhere. Gettysburg, Normandy, Kevin's Front Hall.

"Charlie," Mom said softly. "This is not how I wanted to have this discussion. . . ."

"Well, then you shouldn't be catting around in coat clos-ets with . . ." I interrupted her but she interrupted me back.

"I'm not *catting around*, Charlie. I think I'm falling in . . ."

I grabbed her because at that moment, Kevin turned the

95

corner. His cape fluttered behind him when he stopped short, spotting us. He looked in my eyes and, I felt fairly certain, knew instantly what was going through my mind.

Brad crashed into Kevin from behind, and yelled, "Hey, watch where I'm going, bub!" He smiled broadly, but then, when nobody grinned in return, he asked, "What's going on?"

"Nothing," Kevin and I both said.

"Jinx!" Brad grinned his crazy grin.

"Let's go," Kevin said.

After they passed us, I grabbed my mother and dragged her back into the coat closet. It was the only place to get any privacy in that dumb house, obviously. I shut the door. Mom found a light switch on the wall beside the door.

"Pretty familiar with this coat closet, huh, Mom?"

"Charlie," she said. "Please stop. Listen to me. I see this is making you very uncomfortable, and I'm sorry about that. I know it's surprising—nobody is more surprised than I am, myself. I certainly never planned this, didn't go looking for this. You know me, Charlie. All I wanted was you and me, and American history, some clear nights looking at the lake, and maybe tenure before I turned forty. And I got it; I got all that, and I was completely happy. Or completely satisfied, I should say. But then, well, I've been getting to know Joe . . ."

"Joe," I said, trying to support my woozy self against the wall and knocking over a battalion of umbrellas in the process.

"Yes, Joe," Mom said. "And the strangest thing is happening to me, Charlie. I never thought it would. I thought I was beyond all this craziness. But the truth is, I'm falling in love."

I turned around and smashed my head into the closet wall. Falling in love. My mother. My safe, sane, stable mother. Falling in love? And with Kevin's father? "Why should he buy a cow?" I muttered.

"What?"

"Nothing." I banged my forehead against the wall a little harder.

"Charlie, please. It doesn't take away from my happiness with everything else, it takes away nothing from you . . ."

"From me? I'm not a baby, Mother! Why are you treating me like a baby?" As if I was thinking it was some sort of competition for her affection. That was, like, the one problem I hadn't considered. Well, until she brought it up.

"I'm trying to treat you like an adult."

"Well, you're failing," I said. There was, to be fair, nothing she could do at that moment that would be right.

"Charlie." She reached out to try to gather me in her arms.

She smelled different. Like *him*, I realized. I pulled away. "Don't hug me," I said. "Haven't you done enough groping already in this closet tonight?"

Then she did slap me, smack across the face. "You have no right to talk to me that way, little miss," she spat out, quiet now, angrier than I'd ever seen her. "Not ever."

We stood there face-to-face, both breathing fire. *So, then, I guess I'm really* not *a child anymore,* I thought. That realization hurt as much as my cheek. More. *I am your baby,* I wanted to yell. *You just hit your baby. You are supposed to be an adult, to be strong and selfless and think of how your actions will affect me!* I touched my hot face. When I saw her expression soften with concern, I took the opportunity to spin around and throw the door open.

It smashed Kevin full-force in the face.

His hand was on his cheek like mine was on mine. "And another thing, Kevin," I yelled at him. "If your closet is going to look so much like a bathroom, you ought to put up a sign!"

"What?" He looked baffled.

I stormed past him to his front door, which I tried to yank open. I tugged so hard that I was grunting but it didn't budge. I stamped my foot and cursed, trying not to cry. Beside me, Kevin whispered, "Hey." He reached in front of me and turned the bolt lock. I flung the door open and ran down his front steps and across his damp lawn, to where it was dark.

# fifteen

THE NEXT MORNING I woke up feeling overwhelmingly lonely. Maybe that's how anybody awake at five in the morning feels, when the light is weak and the sky is November pale. I don't know why depression is supposed to be blue. I felt like I had the grays.

After a while I dragged myself out of bed and sat down in front of my computer. Nobody was online yet. Blah. I didn't know what to do. I hated everything. I wished I could just start everything fresh.

*Yes,* I thought, feeling the gray lift slightly. *Maybe that's what I really need, actually.* A fresh start. I did a little surfing and decided Mom and I should move to New Hampshire. That would be a fresh start. I found a real estate site and started checking out houses in southern New Hampshire so

Mom could still commute to work. I would have to switch schools, but, hey, change is good. It would be good for both of us to get away from all this. Maybe we would even buy a non-figurative cow. I could do chores. That would probably be good for me, get my butt in gear. The root of all my problems, I started thinking, might be that I needed a more wholesome, simple, Patagonia-style life.

While I was deciding how many acres we'd need, Tess called.

"I was about to call you," I told her.

"Beat you again."

"Surprise, surprise," I said. "We might move to New Hampshire."

"What? You better be kidding, Charlie."

"We're thinking we might be rural people at heart. You know, since my mom brought up the cow, I've been thinking . . ."

"Oh, please. For a second I thought you were serious."

"I am serious."

"Your mother barely likes to step off the deck. And you are allergic to fur."

"Well," I said, "you can grow out of allergies."

"Your favorite animal is smoked salmon. Come on. I have something serious to ask you."

"New Hampshire is a very serious state," I said. "Do you know what their state motto is? 'Live Free or Die.' Die! It says that on, like, their license plates and stuff. Die. I'm serious." I clicked on a house that had four bedrooms and eight acres, and was actually kind of pretty in a rustic way, if you like snow a lot. I could learn not to hate the cold, maybe. Live Free or Die.

I was about to tell Tess some more facts about New Hampshire—like it is the first state to vote in presidential primaries and it has four nicknames, including the Granite State—when Tess asked, "Do you think I should tell Kevin I love him?"

"No," I said.

"Oh," she said. "That was definite."

"No, I . . ." I wanted to back off my absoluteness and try to breathe and also give myself a chance to think about her, my best friend, instead of just my own sad selfishness. But every cell in my body wanted to scream, NO! You canNOT love him, or it makes me even worse for loving him, too! "Did he say he loves you?" I asked.

How mean is it that I was hoping she would say no?

"No."

I am such a bad friend. I tried to pull down my smile. It was a fight. I wished I could be made of granite. I wanted to be strong and definite and true, to live free or die.

"But do you think the boy has to say it first?" Tess asked.

"No," I said. "Definitely not. But do you? Love him?"

I heard her breathing, in, out. It is my favorite sound, somebody breathing near me, even through the phone.

"I . . ." She hesitated. Tess is always very definite. Tess could be a New Hampshirite. "I think so."

Oh.

"So I guess you guys had some fun after I left."

"Abruptly. Why did you? Somebody said you had a fight with your mom."

"Well . . ." *Tell her.*

"I was like, no way," Tess said. "Charlie and her mom have the perfect relationship."

Did that used to be true? Or was that just one of those fictions Tess made up that I liked to believe even when I knew it wasn't completely true? Either way, I didn't want to correct her right that second. I wasn't sure which of us I was protecting. "I had cramps."

"Oh," she said. "Why didn't you tell me? You know I always have Midol. And I was looking for you. Jennifer said you got a sudden bad headache."

"That, too," I lied. "And I, I leaked."

"Oh," Tess groaned sympathetically. "How awful. Oh, Charlie. Did anybody see?"

"I don't think so."

"Well, that's lucky at least."

"Yeah, I guess."

"If nobody knows," she said, "You can just decide it never happened."

"My theory exactly," I agreed. So she's as dishonest as I am?

"So that's why," she said. "Okay. I just . . ."

"What?"

"I was just surprised when I couldn't find you, and then Jen said you'd left."

"I'm sorry. I should've . . ."

"It just seemed like you would tell me, not Jen. Whatever. George looked sad all night."

"He did? I'm just, I'm sorry. I wasn't thinking, I just had to . . ."

"No, definitely," Tess said.

"Hey," I said. "Let's stop talking about what a jerk I am so you can tell me what happened," I said, flopping down on my bed. "Between you and, you know, Kevin."

"Nothing," she whispered. "Nothing like a big thing or, you know, the pact or like he saved my life or made a grand gesture or anything like that but . . . do you promise you won't think I'm weird?"

"I already think you're weird," I assured her.

"Good point. Okay. When I was getting ready to leave the party, and I had barely talked to him—I was really mad at him because he was ignoring me pretty much the entire party—I walked by him and when he saw me, he smiled. Is that crazy? But it was this gradual smile. It just kind of took its time spreading across his face. He just looked at me like he was really happy to see me and, like, he thought I looked, I don't know, good."

Well.

"Charlie?"

"Ungh."

"Is that ridiculous?"

"Nuh-uh."

"At that moment I knew, I just knew that I loved him. I

103

almost said it right then and there but then I thought, whoa, slow down, better talk to Charlie first. Because this is . . . I don't want to mess it up."

"No," I said, managing to blink. My eyeballs were parched.

"So you think I should wait, then? I'm being a doink, right?"

"No, you're not," I said. "Not at all. That sounds . . . I don't blame you at all."

"Really? It's romantic, right?"

"Yes," I said.

"I knew you would get it. I would never even try to explain to anybody else how this one smile just about broke all my ribs. Only you. We're so lucky, aren't we? I mean, people like Darlene, who do they tell everything to?"

"Tess," I said. "I have to . . ." . . . *tell you something, some things, some stuff I should have been telling you all along. . . .*

"I have to go, too," she said. "See you in school tomorrow. I feel so much better. Is that weird? Maybe I didn't have to tell him I love him; I just had to tell somebody. No—I just had to tell you. Thanks, Charlie."

She hung up before I could say you're welcome. I hung up, too, and since I couldn't even move off my bed, never mind to another state, I just lay there a hundred miles away from New Hampshire, until the phone in my hand rang again.

# sixteen

"HI, IT'S GEORGE."

"Hi," I said.

"We have to talk."

I hate when people say that. Even George.

"Why?" I asked. I was pretty talked out from the last phone call.

"Because sign language over the phone really sucks," he said.

I smiled.

"Yes, like that. Can't read you there."

"I was smiling," I told him.

"Oh. Okay. So. Um, obviously it's not working out."

"What isn't?"

"Us," he said.

I sat up. *Are you dumping me?* I thought, but what I said was, "Oh."

"So," he said. "Okay?"

"Okay," I said.

"So, see ya."

"I guess," I answered.

"By the way—I knew that people sometimes put out plastic flamingoes on their lawns."

"Oh," I said. *What?*

He didn't hang up but he didn't say anything else, so I hung up. Then I flopped back down on my bed and cried. Not just about the humiliation of being tossed, but also about George, and how I had totally messed up my relationship with him when he is such a great guy and I am such an undeserving heap of poop. Then I cried about Kevin, and how he only used me when he really loved Tess all along, looking at her all happy to see her and like she looks good. Then I cried about Tess, and why does she get to be prettier than me and more confident and fun, and also what a bad friend I am to her, lusting after her boyfriend and keeping secrets from her when I know she would never do that to me. And then, just for good measure, I cried about nobody loving me best in the world since my father has his cute new family and always has to take a deep breath before he says a word to disorderly me, and my mother of all people (ha!) is all dreamy-eyed about some man and if they get married it won't just be me and her anymore, looking at the lake; it will be him and her, with me probably shunted upstairs to play with the other kids.

The other kids being a brilliant little girl and, oh yeah, the crush of my life.

After that I was so dehydrated I needed to drink an entire liter of seltzer. I didn't even have to pee, after. That's how much I had cried.

Then I cut up a cucumber and put the slices on my eyes. I had read about doing that in a magazine Tess and I stole from her oldest sister, Isabel. It was an article called "The Best Revenge Is Looking Good." We almost got caught in our theft, we were snorting so loud at the stupidity of it all. Who'd lie around with cucumber slices on her eyes, if she weren't a dead fish on a platter at a catered brunch? For that matter, who'd cry her eyes out all night just because a boy dumped you?

A Pop-Tart, that's who. What I always swore I'd never stoop to become.

I gave myself a stern talking to: Get over yourself, honey. Get some perspective on world events and real tragedy, huh?

So then I cried a little about what a shallow jerk I am.

I lay back down on the couch like a smoked trout. The cucumbers felt surprisingly refreshing. Maybe it would not be so bad to be an entrée.

I noticed that with my eyes covered my hearing was particularly acute. I heard Mom walk into the living room but pretended not to, until she asked, "What are you doing?"

"Nothing," I answered casually.

I listened to her sitting down in a chair, which scraped a bit on the floor.

"Tuesday night," she said, "we're going to have dinner with Joe, Kevin, and Samantha. I was thinking Mama Mexico might be fun."

I sat up and the cucumbers fell, one on the floor and one on the couch. "Mom!"

"You know, there's music, and I thought Samantha might enjoy that lady who makes the balloon animals."

"I'm not going," I said.

"Charlotte. Come on. We're better than this, you and I."

"It's not . . . Mom, I honestly don't care about your personal life," I said in my most blasé voice. "Do what you want. But Tuesday I'm busy."

"What?"

"Newspaper. Don't you remember? I'm on the City News staff. I told you. Weren't you listening?"

"Yes," Mom said, "I know." She was talking in her *I'm so reasonable* voice. I hate that voice. "We would have dinner after that, in the evening."

"I'll have homework." I put a fresh couple of cucumber slices on my eyes and lay back down.

She just sat there not making a sound while I counted silently. I swore to myself I would not cave in and take off the cucumbers before a hundred at the earliest. At eighty-three I heard the chair squeak and her footsteps leaving the room.

I sat up, dumping the new pair of cukes. "I get a lot of homework this year, you know! Plus the whole journalism responsibility! What if there's some . . . news? In the city? I might have to go out and cover it!"

Nothing.

I immediately thought of ten obnoxious things to yell but I knew she'd just ignore them so I didn't waste my breath. I was considering getting really annoyed that she was acting so unimpressed with my single-minded devotion to my newspaper career, until I admitted to myself that so far I hadn't done anything other than download phone numbers for the Board of Ed, and complain about how boring it was.

I moved on to Best Revenge/Looking Good plans. There was very little I could do right then to make a positive difference in the world, I rationalized, and though I had always thought of myself as a good person, I was evidently wrong, as even George had figured out. I might however be able to perk up my looks marginally. Maybe that was a way I could contribute to making the world a better place, a more beautiful place.

I knew that was a load of crap even as I thought it, and so it was with complete self-loathing that I marched into the kitchen with a recipe for apricot/egg facial mask to continue attempting to improve myself superficially.

# seventeen

EVERY TIME I saw George he looked away from me. I tried to be casual as I spied around corners, trying to catch him popping up at some other girl's locker. I'd scratch her eyes out.

I had a heck of a nerve being jealous, of course, but there you have it. The pope is unlikely to beatify me soon, in any event. He didn't seem to be otherwise engaged, though, just going about his business. George, that is. The pope doesn't go to my school.

Tess was back to talking more about training for a triathlon than about love, which was a relief. I may even have agreed to train with her, in my fit of gratitude at not hearing the name *Kevin* and the verb *love* in the same sentence.

I smiled at Kevin once, briefly, outside English, thinking

purposefully: *No matter what, I will not reveal my secret to you.* This is another tip I got from Tess's sister Isabel's magazine. Have a secret; don't reveal it. It matters not at all what your secret is. My secret was my middle name—Reese.

Kevin didn't seem particularly intrigued.

After school the next afternoon, at newspaper, I was sitting next to Penelope, keeping a running tab of how many times she sighed (fourteen) on the top corner of my math homework and trying not to stare at Kevin, when Mr. McKinley stomped toward us.

"Charles," he boomed, meaning me.

I twitched to show I had heard. Or maybe in fear. I was still unable to function near him.

"When you go to the next Board of Ed meeting, make sure your notes are good. Right?"

I nodded. So Penelope had told him what a disaster my notes were on the first one, obviously. The rat.

"You don't want to misquote a Board of Ed member, right?"

I shook my head, proud of my impressive muscular control. How humiliating. It was my first time ever writing a newspaper article—maybe I could get a little instruction or support? Especially because, hello, I am not even interested in newspaper. I am here by accident!

"Where do you think we get our funding?" McKinley bellowed.

A problem: It is hard to answer a non–yes/no question

with only slight head movements. I thought for a moment. Where do we get our funding? Our what? There was a buzzing sound in my head. What was the question?

"The Board of Ed," he answered himself. Hard to tell if he was happy or pissed. He sounded both. I was staring at his scuffed brown shoes. They were fancier than you'd guess for a guy that big and gruff who walks tilted forward at about a forty-degree angle.

In case he was waiting for me to say something, I nodded slightly.

"But be impartial," he bellowed, then turned to make sure everybody could hear him. In all of New England, maybe. "You cover your benefactors the same as anybody else. You must be fair, unbiased, objective. Because what is the most important element in a free society?"

"A free press!" everybody answered. Everybody except me.

McKinley clapped me on the shoulder with his meaty hand and stomped away as the late bell rang. I was in such a rush to get the heck out of there, I almost crashed into Kevin in the doorway.

"Sorry," I said.

"See ya," he said. "Later."

"My middle name is Reese," I blurted.

"What?"

"That's my . . ." What was I doing? "That's a secret." Ugh. I used to be within the spectrum of normal. "Don't tell anyone," I added feebly.

"Okay," he said. "It's your mother's last name, right?"

I nodded. He knows stuff about me. I felt kind of naked and kind of scared and kind of, simultaneously, electrified. "That's right," I whispered.

"My father mentioned . . ." His voice trailed off. "Well, see you tonight, I guess."

# eighteen

THE MARIACHI BAND started playing right around the moment when Kevin's father first mentioned Vermont. Until that moment it had been possible to pretend this was just one of those awkward/tedious dinners parents arrange so they can chat with each other and simultaneously pretend they are spending time with their children, because their children are around the same ages as each other and wouldn't it be fun if they hit it off? I've endured these dinners with my mother's college roommates and my father's friends from the club. I know how to do it; you just smile a lot and say, "Oh, that's great" and "Thank you" whenever you hear your name, and otherwise you are basically free to space out.

That's how I was treating this dinner. Kevin, I decided, is just the son of my mother's friend.

But then the mariachi band came over and started playing "La Bamba," and Kevin's father put his arm around my mother and said, "Over Christmas break we're going up to Vermont."

"Vermont?" my mother asked. "Oh, how wonderful."

I shot her a look, chastising her for the false cheer. Ew.

"Oh, it is," said Joe. "It's wonderful. It's on Sun-up Mountain, and it's just this really cozy house. It belongs to my parents but they rarely use it these days. I love it there. So do Kevin and Samantha. It's just great. We ski all day, build a fire afterward, just relax. Charlie, do you ski?"

"Yeah," I said, feeling my face get red.

"Kevin is a great skier," his father bragged. "And Samantha's really learning, too."

Samantha sipped her Shirley Temple and looked from face to face.

"Hey," Joe said. "You two should come!"

"Well," said Mom, all coy. "Charlie is supposed to be going to her father's over Christmas this year."

"Yeah," I said. Then muttered, as I always do, "Unfortunately."

"You can see she's thrilled about it," Mom said, instead of telling me not to be rude. "It really is very boring for her down at the Cape over Christmas. Actually, her father and I have been discussing maybe switching holidays, and I could have Charlie over Christmas and he could have her over Thanksgiving . . ."

"Am I involved in these negotiations at all?" I asked. "Or am I just a geranium you two pass back and forth?"

Mom smiled at me like a TV mom on a commercial about her rascally kid who has fully recovered from her cough. "You are a geranium."

"That would be great, wouldn't it, kids?" Mr. Lazarus asked his children. "Elizabeth and Charlie should come with us. Don't you think so?"

"Yes," Samantha answered obediently, and smiled sweetly at me. "You could sleep in my room. Kevin and I each have two beds in our rooms. Unless, I mean, I know you're his friend, but . . ."

Mr. Lazarus chuckled his deep chuckle. "She'll stay in your room, sweetheart," he told his daughter.

I put on a fake smile and said to my mother, "And where will you be sleeping, Mom?"

"Well," she said. "I . . ."

"Interesting question," Kevin said.

I was too furious with my mother to thank him for the compliment.

"She could have my room," said Mr. Lazarus. "And I would bunk in with Kevin. Of course."

"Of course," Mom said. "Well, let's take it slow and think this through. It's a very nice invitation. Thank you, Joe. There's a lot to consider and it's just an idea. . . ."

The band, by then, had wandered over to our table. They started playing the "Mexican Hat Dance." Really loud. I crossed my arms over my chest and slumped in my chair, grimacing, waiting for these sweaty men to finish blaring their insipid song in my ears. When they did, Mr. Lazarus handed them a tip and they went on to the next table.

"Think about it," said Mr. Lazarus. "I bet you would love Vermont, both of you. And we'd love to have you. Right, kids?"

"Right," chimed Samantha.

"Bull," said Kevin.

We all stared at him.

"Kevin," his father chided.

"What a load of crap, Dad," Kevin said. "Why do you have to lie to us? Put on this whole charade, as if you and Elizabeth hadn't planned this, as if it hadn't already all been discussed and agreed on by the two of you—as if we 'kids' had any say in it at all! Maybe Samantha is naïve enough to fall for that but not me and Charlie."

Okay, I had fallen for it, or at least hadn't been focused on that aspect of the situation, but no way was I opening my mouth and admitting it.

"Kevin," his father said. "How about you calm down and we can . . ."

Kevin stood up. His chair almost smashed into the waitress behind him, who was balancing the tray with all our plates on it. "Calm down, my ass."

"Kevin!"

"For once I would so love," Kevin said, as the waitress put

down his sizzling chicken fajitas, "some honesty. Everyone always makes excuses and hides behind convenient little stories—why doesn't anybody just stand up and say this is what I want, or this is what I think? Everybody is so . . ."

"So . . . what?" Mr. Lazarus asked, his smile hardening slightly.

"So compromised."

"Sit down, please, Kev, and eat your dinner."

He shoved his chair toward the table. "Come on, Charlie."

I had a barbecued rib in my mouth. I put it down, chewed quickly while wiping my mouth on my napkin, grabbed my bag, and followed him out. I was mad, too. I didn't even say excuse me as I left.

We stomped across the parking lot. There was a Dumpster there, which Kevin punched. It was very loud and left a slight dent. He turned his back to me. I wasn't sure if I should ask if he was all right or if I should wait silently or go back to the restaurant alone.

"I don't even care if he and she are, you know."

I didn't answer. He sounded like he was trying not to cry.

"But they could have the courage to be honest about it. Do you know what I mean? About honesty?"

"Yeah," I lied.

He turned around. "They lie and lie and lie—they don't even realize they're doing it. But they'll do anything to avoid a confrontation."

"Our parents?"

"All of them," he said. "Adults. Most people."

I nodded.

"But not you," he said. "You don't shy away from anything."

"Me?" Good golly, the queen of conflict-averse.

He shook his head. "You're different. That's what's so cool about you."

"It is?"

"For a while I thought you were stuck-up. But then I realized it was just me, specifically, you were nasty to."

"I was not!"

"Don't start lying now, too. You know you were."

"Not always," I mumbled.

"No," he whispered. "Not always."

Whoa, Nelly! Take a breath and BACK OFF. "Maybe I'm just nasty," I suggested.

"Maybe." A hint of a smile lifted one side of his mouth. "But I think you're probably the most honest person I know. I like that about you."

I shrugged, unable to speak. I would never do anything to hurt Tess. My friendship with her is the most important relationship in my life with the possible—possible—exception of my mother. At the same time, there I was in the parking lot, really, really wanting to kiss my best friend's boyfriend. How's that for honest?

A car sped past on the road. I resisted the urge to turn

and look at it, as I was resisting every other urge. I decided to stay completely still, to wait and see what he did first: my feeble attempt at maintaining my innocence.

His cell phone rang, which broke the tension. He took it out of his pocket, looked at it, then turned it toward me. The caller ID said TESS. I raised my eyebrows at him. He shrugged and let it ring until it stopped ringing. He kept it in his palm then, as if he was wondering what else it might start to do. But it just lay there, still as a rock. We both watched it. When the ringing started again, neither of us was surprised, until he looked at it and said, "It's not mine."

Digging through my bag, I realized it was of course Tess, calling me; I got to the phone in time to confirm it. I showed it to Kevin and didn't answer either.

"You, uh . . ." he said after a while, in his low, raspy voice. "You know we have no say in this Vermont trip."

"Yup," I said, and cleared my throat. "You know what the state motto is, of Vermont?"

"No."

"Exactly," I said.

He didn't laugh. He slipped his cell phone back into his pocket.

"How's your hand?"

"Fine. My hand?"

"That Dumpster had it coming," I said. "After how it acted toward you."

"What?"

"Nothing," I said, putting my cell away, too. "It's freezing out here."

"Yeah," he said.

We started walking back toward the restaurant. I was really cold and still pretty hungry but I also wasn't completely ready to go back to our parents.

"Can I ask you a question?" I asked, which of course was itself a question.

"Sure," he said, shoving his hands into his pockets.

"Is your mother . . ."

"I don't want to talk about my mother."

"Okay," I said. We walked some more. When we got to the door he opened it, and since I thought he might be holding it open for me I started to walk through. But he wasn't, so we kind of crashed into each other. I said sorry and we headed toward our table, where a lady was making a balloon hat shaped like a flower garden for Kevin's father, and where my mother had icicles behind her smile.

It was a long dinner and a longer ride home. Halfway home my mother said, without taking her eyes off the road, "You are never to leave the table like that again. I don't like the way Kevin spoke to his father or the assumptions either of you were making. It is insulting and inappropriate."

I slumped down in my seat and flipped on the seat warmer. "Sorry."

"If we do go to Vermont, which will be MY decision, I will expect you to behave yourself."

"You sound like Dad."

"You sound like . . . never mind." She took a few deep breaths.

We drove along in silence for a while. I got to picturing how it would be in Vermont, spending the week there with Kevin and his family—skiing together, eating together, waiting for each other to finish in the bathroom. No way. How could she do this to me? What if she really does make me do this? How could I survive it? So I asked, "Can I bring a friend?" I was just thinking Tess always eases the tension, like when I drag her down to the Cape sometimes for my weekends with Dad. But then I immediately thought, well, maybe not Tess. Maybe Jennifer would be better. Or does that make me an evil person?

But anyway, Mom said, "I don't think so, Charlie. There isn't room and—Charlie, listen. I think the idea Joe had, and I had, that we had, is to spend some time, the five of us."

That took my breath away, and not just the admission that Kevin was right, that this idea had been discussed already and hatched between my mother and his father. It was the other part—what that meant, spend some time, the five of us. Why? Oh, no. "Really?"

"Really," she said, her eyes still fixed straight ahead, into the darkness.

# nineteen

"HELLO?"

"Hi," I said. "Tess."

"Charlie! I am so glad you called. You weren't online last night and I tried to call your cell but I think it was dead or something."

I looked out the kitchen window toward the lake. Rain was coming down hard on a slant. "Tess, last night . . ."

"I was thinking I won't ride today because of the rain. Do you want to do something after school? You could, like, wait for me while I do chorus and we could take the late bus home together? Maybe to your house, and I could flirt with Kevin a little and you could tell me what you think."

"About what?"

"If you think I'm doing it well. Because I think I

might be messing it up."

"I'm sure you're not messing it up."

"I don't know how to do it like the Pop-Tarts."

"You're better than they are," I assured her. "The Pop-Tarts wish they could be you."

"Really?"

"Yes. You're smarter than they are, more talented, prettier, and more confident. Everybody wants to be you."

"That's just because everybody wants to be going out with Kevin lately."

"True," I admitted. "No, I mean, that's not the only reason . . ."

"Right." Tess grunted. "Don't you hate sweaters with too-small head holes? Do I have a grotesquely large head?"

"No." I grabbed my jacket off the hook.

"Do you think me and Kevin will last as long as you and George will?"

Oops, another thing I'd forgotten to tell her. I honestly used to be a good friend. I sat down on the bench and said, "He dumped me."

"Who?"

"George."

"No way."

"Yup," I said. "On the phone."

Tess gasped. "When?"

"Last night." Close enough.

"You didn't even call me?"

"It was . . . late, and I . . ." *am a lousy friend* . . .

"Oh, man! That's why you weren't picking up? Charlie, you need to lean on your friends, not go sulk by yourself! Is that what you were trying to tell me before? I am so sorry, Charlie. I'm so selfish. Can you forgive me?"

"Yeah," I said. "It's not . . ."

"Wait—is this like New Hampshire?"

"You mean cold?"

"I mean a joke. Are you just joking? About George?"

"No," I said. "He said it wasn't working out. What do you think that means?"

"It means he's hooking up with somebody else."

"You think?"

"I'll kill her," Tess said. "The little tart. Is it a Pop-Tart? I can't believe George Jacobson is such a shallow pig!"

"I think he just stopped liking me."

"That can't be it," Tess said. "Who would not like you?"

"George, I guess."

"Then he's an idiot."

*Who needs boys?* I thought. "Thanks."

"So, anyway, will you?"

"Will I what?" I stood up to zip my coat. I had to hurry or I'd miss the bus.

"Stay after? I need your unbiased judgment on this."

"Why do you think you're messing up your flirtation with Kevin? Did something happen?" I prayed that didn't sound like I was hoping.

"I don't know," she sighed. "He is a little . . . we had sort of a fight, I think, online last night."

"Last night?"

"Yeah, at like eleven. He was just all cranky and, I don't know, nasty, critical. Cryptic. You know?"

"Yeah," I said. We both thought about Kevin for a bit.

"Maybe I just overreact," Tess suggested. "I get so mad at him, but do you think maybe it's because I've never felt this way about . . ."

"Hey," I interrupted. "Remember you said his mother . . ."

"Charlie, I'm serious. Will you stay after with me? We can do whatever you want after, I promise. Please?"

"I have to go to the Board of Ed meeting tonight," I remembered.

"Seriously? Why?"

"Newspaper. It's my assignment."

"Again?"

"Every month."

"Yuck," she said. "Sure, okay. I'll go with you."

"Really? It's incredibly boring."

"That's why they're called the School Bored, right?"

"Thanks," I said. "Um . . ." *Hey, did I mention that my mom is going out with . . .*

"You okay?" she asked.

"What do you mean?"

"You know, about George. That is so weird."

"Oh, George," I said, remembering. "Yeah, I guess."

"Well, be strong, pal. He'll come crawling back."

"Thanks." It is sometimes surprisingly hard to be best friends with a person you wish you could be. "Really, Tess. Thanks."

"Guys are so strange."

"Yeah," I said. "Kind of like girls."

"Too true," said Tess.

# twenty

SCHOOL WENT BY numbingly as usual, except that Tess stuck close and gave poor George the evil eye all day. Jennifer and Darlene joined in at lunch, telling me he was just a jerk. When I told them that no, he was right, I had been pretty lousy to him, Tess said it just proves how stupid he was to dump me when even as the injured party I had the generosity to defend him. Jennifer is the only one who stopped at that point. On the way to our lockers afterward, she said, "That's true, actually. You were pretty mean to him."

Tess whispered to me later that I shouldn't be mad at Jennifer for saying that because it was probably just that Jennifer is always cranky when we can't go out at lunch on rainy days. I wasn't mad.

After school, while Jennifer went to the gym for practice

and Tess went to the chorus room and Kevin and George were both down at band, I sat in the lobby and watched the rain. I knew I should get my homework done because I was going to cover the meeting that night, but I spaced out instead.

Tess picked me up at the end of the period and we put on our jackets slowly, waiting for the band kids to get out. When they did, George smiled at me but then stopped himself. "Hi," I said. I couldn't help it. Tess was practically growling at the poor guy.

"Hi," he said. "See ya. Nice weather, huh?"

"Yeah," I said. I wanted to say something lighthearted, both to show that I was just fine, thank you, not crushed by his rejection, and also to show that we could be friends. And also a little bit to remind him what he had thrown away—a witty girl, a funny girl, a girl who could make him laugh on a stormy day. So here is the hilarious verbal joust I came up with: "See ya."

Kevin passed us, drumming on his jeans. We followed him out. Well, we had to get to the bus, too, and by then our jackets were on.

George splashed through a puddle, running with his trumpet case over his head to his mom's car. I think she might have waved at me. Even his mother is nice. I waved back and followed Tess onto the bus.

She slid into a seat across the aisle from Kevin. I sat down next to her. An awkward moment: How could she flirt with him when I was a boulder between them? But if I made a thing out of switching seats, well, how uncool and embarrassing.

I opened my eyes wide at her.

She shrugged.

In a slightly loud voice, I said, "Tess, would you mind switching seats with me? I get bus-sick if I'm not next to the window."

I heard her make a little squelching-the-laugh noise before she said, "Why sure, Charlie. No problem at all."

By then neither of us could keep from cracking up, especially once she started climbing over me. She clonked me in the ear with her book bag on her way. So when she turned her head away from me and said in a surprised voice, "Oh, Kevin, I didn't see you there!" you can just imagine. We were doubled over in fits of laughter, with tears running down our faces and horrible snorting noises coming out of both of us. We are just lucky we didn't wet our pants.

We got off the bus at my stop, which is a few before Kevin's, tumbling out practically on top of each other in the pouring rain. We had to kind of hold each other up to walk down the hill to my house, and every time one of us was about to gain some control, the other would say, "Oh, Kevin!" and we'd both die all over again.

# twenty-one

I COULDN'T EVEN tell what subject the Board of Ed people were discussing. Well, part of the problem was that I kept falling asleep. Another part of the problem was that Tess, who was fast asleep in the seat beside me, was snoring at top volume, which made it hard to hear. I raised my eyebrows in an attempt to keep my eyelids from closing, and told myself *pay attention, pay attention*. In the special reporter's notebook Mom bought me, my hand wrote down the random words I heard through my semiconscious haze. When the tall bald guy in the center of the little stage bellowed, "All in favor?" I snapped awake and realized I'd missed yet another section.

I bit my cheek, pinched my wrist, promised myself I'd catch the whole next issue and focus the nugget on that, and then plunged numbly into la-la land again until the next gavel hit.

Chairs squeaked, people murmured, and I jolted awake. The meeting had ended and my notes were nonexistent. Uh-oh. On the plus side, I had not gotten such deep sleep in months, and felt very well rested.

"What am I going to do?" I whispered to Tess. "I kept falling asleep."

"Really?" Tess asked. "I'll tell you what happened. Elephants will be the new cafeteria monitors starting in . . ."

I shoved her. "Thanks anyway."

"Interview somebody," she suggested.

I turned to the lady standing beside me. "Excuse me," I said in my most polite voice. "I am a reporter for the high school newspaper. What would you say was the most important thing that happened in tonight's meeting?"

The lady smiled. "I thought my husband spoke well," she said, and rushed away from me.

I looked at Tess.

"Follow her," she whispered.

"Ma'am?" I asked, chasing her up the aisle. First time in my life I ever called anyone *ma'am*. I felt like I was in a Tennessee Williams play. "Which was your husband's speech?"

She turned around. She had on a pink sweater set and a double strand of pearls. She smiled again, the exact same smile as last time. "He's the superintendent of schools, Mr. Buckley."

I wrote that down in my notebook, nodding as I wrote, which severely taxed my limited skills of coordination, because I was standing up at the same time. "Was he the, um . . ."—*Don't say bald guy, don't say bald guy . . .* —"gentleman seated in the center of the, um, thing?"

"Dais, yes."

I wrote down *day-is. Bald. Buckley. Super.* I gave up on nodding because I almost dropped the pad. But she had stopped talking so I said, "And?"

"And?"

"And what would you say was the essence of his speech?"

"Were you that girl who was snoring, then?" Mrs. Buckley asked.

"Um," I answered, thinking, forget journalism. There must be something less boring that I could force myself to be passionate about. I mean, other than passion itself. "Well, I . . ."

"No," Tess answered, behind Mrs. Buckley. "That was me. She was wide awake. She just wants to liven up her piece with some interviews of the crowd. It's her first article for the high school newspaper. She's very diligent."

"Mm-hmm," said Mrs. Buckley. "Well, I think Mr. Buckley made a very convincing case about eliminating funding for those minor afterschool programs that benefit few students. Don't you?"

"Which programs?" I asked her.

"Well, not newspaper, of course, and not real sports. The

examples Mr. Buckley gave were, let me remember, the anarchy club, which has no members . . ."

I had to smile at that.

"Yes, that got a nice laugh the first time, too."

Chastised, I lowered my head and wrote. *Anarchy club. No membs.*

"Oh," she said. "Also the Frisbee team. They've never gone to a single game, or match, or whatever it is you are supposed to do with a Frisbee team."

"Mmm," I said, still writing *cut funding Frisbee team never match.*

"Anyhow, his proposal to take a careful look at the extracurricular budget was unanimously approved, and I think that was the most important thing accomplished at tonight's meeting. That's my opinion. Others may think the tax report was more important, but truthfully I may have dozed off for a moment during that one."

I smiled at her. "Thank you, Mrs. Buckley."

"Oh." She frowned. I frowned, too. "Please don't use my name for attribution."

"Yes, ma'am," I said. "Strictly off the record." Smiles all around.

"It is nice to see children involved in the process," she said. "This is the kind of extracurricular activity that really does deserve funding. And your name is?"

"Her name is Tess," Tess told her before I could say my name. "And my name is Charlotte Collins. But it's not my fault I fell asleep. It's a medical condition."

Mrs. Buckley looked concerned. Tess smiled at her angelically. I shoved Tess out of there before she could engage the superintendent's wife in any further fictions.

"How was it?" Mom asked.

"I don't know," I answered honestly.

"So evasive," Mom answered. We walked out to the car. Mom was humming softly to herself. She never used to do that.

# twenty-two

THEY PRINTED MY byline.

Not only that, but all seven people who read my article seemed to like it. I took that as a huge success and was feeling good about myself until everything fell apart at lunch.

People Who Commented Favorably:
1. Mom ("It's great. Really well written.")
2. Tess ("Sounds like you were actually conscious during that meeting.")
3. Jennifer ("Strong work.")
4. Darlene ("Wow. I didn't know you were smart, too!")
5. Penelope ("Better. But nobody reads the City News, anyway.")
6. Mr. McKinley ("That's a solid bit of reporting, Charles.")

7. George ("What if the anarchists organize a protest?")
People Who Didn't Comment at All:
1. Kevin
2. Everybody else

Despite that small disappointment, I was feeling pretty darned happy all day. My name was in print, my article was a solid bit of reporting, I had actually accomplished something. Maybe newspaper was not so bad. Maybe there is more to it than just stalking my best friend's boyfriend.

Life was good.

Until, as I mentioned, lunch.

It was drizzling out—not enough to imprison us all in the cafeteria for the entire forty-two minutes but enough so that Tess and I were kind of unenthusiastic about sitting on the steps to watch Jennifer and the boys shoot hoops. The Pop-Tarts were inside, whispering; the band people were practicing because it was a Thursday; the smokers (including, I noticed, Darlene) were off smoking on the Bridge; the brains were wherever they go at lunch, the library maybe; and we in-betweeners were in between, hovering under the overhang outside the cafeteria.

Kevin tapped me and Tess on the shoulders. We turned toward each other, to look at him. He had come up from behind us.

"Hi," we all said at the same time.

Then nobody said anything for a long minute so I said, too loud, "Ain't lunch fun?"

They both looked at me like I had startled them. Tess smiled and turned to Kevin. "How was band?" she asked in a quiet voice, leaning toward him. There was clearly nothing wrong with her flirting technique.

"Okay," he said, leaning toward her in return.

I thought I should get out of there. Nothing fun about being number three when one and two are flirting. I said, "So . . ." in preparation to wander inside and look for the brains, thinking maybe I could be a brain. I'm not exceptionally smart but maybe if I dedicate myself to schoolwork I could achieve. I could end up a professor like my mother. Oh, joy. "Think I'll . . ."

"Is that a new ski jacket?" Tess asked Kevin.

"Got it last night."

"Nice," Tess told him. "Don't you think, Charlie?"

"As rarely as possible." It was a nice jacket. His shoulders looked even broader than usual.

"The key to her success," Tess explained to Kevin, then turned to me. "Kevin's going skiing over Christmas vacation."

"She knows," Kevin said.

"She does?" Tess asked him. "You know?" she asked me. I shrugged.

"Don't you wish you could go skiing?" Tess smiled at me, then at Kevin. "I have to go to my grandmother's in Baltimore, which is bad enough, but Charlie's spending Christmas break at her father's on the Cape. Some people think the Cape is romantic at Christmas but really it's just cold and damp, right, Charlie?"

"Right," I muttered.

Kevin was squinting at me, like he was trying to figure out something. "She doesn't know?" he asked me.

"Know what?" Tess asked.

I didn't say anything.

"I just . . . she doesn't know?" he repeated.

"Is somebody going to tell me what I don't know, please?" Tess asked.

"I'm not going to my dad's over Christmas vacation," I told Tess. Or rather I told Tess's shoes.

"No, no, no, no. Did something happen?" Tess grabbed me by my shoulders. "Charlie, what happened? Did something happen to your father?"

"No," I said. "My mother."

I looked up at Tess. Her face had gone ashy white. "What? Something's wrong with your mom? Oh, Charlie . . ."

"No," I said.

Tess whipped around to Kevin. "What is going on? Tell me."

"Her mother," Kevin said, and glanced over at me. Tess's hands were still on my shoulders. "My dad and her mother are in . . ." He stopped. He shrugged at me. Tess looked back at me.

"In something," I said, trying to smile, trying to make it fun, funny, a quirky funny thing we could all join together to laugh about at my mother's expense. "In-volved. In cahoots. In . . ."

"Love," Kevin said.

Well, there's a word to put a damper on a rollicking good time.

"They're in love?" Tess asked me.

"That's what my dad said, anyway." Kevin kicked the toe of his work boot into the concrete. "So we're all going away together over Christmas vacation. Skiing. In Vermont."

Tess's hands slid off my shoulders, down my arms, to her sides. "Obviously you knew this. Both of you."

Kevin shrugged. "I figured you knew, too."

"Yes," Tess said. "I'm sure you did. Why wouldn't I know that? You're my, well, whatever, supposedly, and Charlie is my best friend. Supposedly."

She turned around and stomped into the building, leaving me out in the rain with Kevin.

# twenty-three

MY FATHER STARTED driving me nuts as soon as I got to his house the day before Thanksgiving, and by Saturday afternoon was showing no sign of letting up at all. Any time I flopped down to rest briefly between chores, he peppered me with questions: How's your mother? What's she up to these days? Has she fixed the flooding in the basement of that house yet? (Always "that house.") So who's this new friend your mother has?

It took all the way until Friday afternoon to get to that one, the money question. Mom's new "friend."

I shrugged.

"I have a new friend," ABC said.

"Lucky you," I said. I actually do like my half brother, and if he weren't four years old I would swear he knew he was helping me out, deflecting attention. "Tell me about your friend, ABC."

"O-tay."

"Is it a boy or a girl?"

"Actually, I have nineteen friends. Because there are nineteen children in my tlass and I am friends with all nineteen, including, of tourse, myself."

I love that all his Cs sound like Ts. "That's awesome, ABC. Good for you."

He snuggled next to me on the couch. He was warm. This, right here, I decided, this is as much cuteness and love—as much boy—as I could possibly need in this life. He was solid and soft and wearing overalls and a white turtleneck. I was completely fulfilled. So what if Tess still hadn't called me back?

"You're not me," ABC told me.

"No," I said, thinking, *unfortunately*. If I were you I would be sweet and innocent and good and loved. I'd have nineteen friends instead of zero.

"And I'm not you," he said, looking up at me with eyes bigger than his head. "So you don't know what I'm thinking right now."

I gave him a little tickle on his ribs. "You're thinking how much you love me, I bet."

"No," he said, wiggling away slightly. "I'm not."

Dad chuckled.

I sighed. "So what are you thinking, you little stinker?"

Could he tell I loved him so much? I guess not really. He's not me, either.

"I don't have to tell you."

"No." I put my face down in his hair and smelled him, sweet and sweaty. "You don't."

He leaned against me again. "But I'll tell you anyway. I was thinking about when my teacher called me Alexander on the first day. Isn't that funny?"

"Well," I said. "That is your name."

Frown. "No. My name is ABC."

"Those are your initials," I told him, sweetly. "ABC stands for the great and fabulous Alexander Brian Collins."

He kicked me.

"Ouch!"

"No!"

"Ow!"

More kicks, and some punches. "ABC is my really name!"

"I was just . . ."

He head butted me in the stomach. "You doody-dum-dum!"

"Suzie," Dad yelled. "Can't you control him?"

Suzie glared at Dad and scooped up ABC, who really started screaming. "Can't you . . ." Suzie started, but stopped herself, sucking in on her lips. ABC reared his head up and slammed it into her chin. She winced and started making an F sound.

This was something new.

But before she could get any further into the word than that initial sound, she spun around and charged out of the living room, struggling to contain ABC who was in full tantrum mode—red in the face and pounding Suzie with all his little limbs at once. He screamed back to me, "I am very sad and angry at you, doody-dum-dum!"

Which left me alone with Dad and his half-finished leftover turkey sandwich.

"Sorry," I said.

Dad groaned.

"We've been down this road a few times. Should've named the kid Gus."

"Yeah."

He rolled his eyes and I smiled at him. It was the first time I felt like he and I were on the same side, ever.

"So, Charlotte . . ."

"Mm-hmm?" I was hoping we could continue on that track. It would be so cool if he'd say something like *doesn't everybody suck?*

"How's soccer going?"

"I'm not—Dad, I told you, I'm not doing soccer." Not this again.

"Fourteen is a little young to specialize, Char." He winked. "Waiting for basketball, huh?"

"No," I said. I hated this conversation. "I'm not doing basketball either."

"Come on, are you lazy? Or a baby? You afraid you won't

make the team? Is that what you're afraid of? Come on, put on your sneakers and let's go practice. By the time you go back they'll make you a starter." He stood up. "Who's the coach? Is it still Jim Duffy?"

"I don't know, Dad."

"You just gonna waste your whole high school time moping around the house reading poetry? Do you know what college costs? Do you even care about trying to get an athletic scholarship?"

"I will never get an athletic scholarship, Dad!"

"Not moping around like a geek, you won't!"

"I am not a jock," I yelled. "Maybe you'll have more success with Gus, if you stick around long enough!"

"Who's Gus?" Suzie asked, standing in the doorway.

Dad and I looked at her and both cracked up a little. "Old friend of mine," he said, back on my side.

"Mommy!" ABC yelled from upstairs. "How many more minutes?"

"Seven," Suzie bellowed, and went back up the stairs.

Dad sat back down and took a huge bite of his sandwich. I could hear the mantel clock ticking.

"The house looks nice," I offered. "As always."

He brushed crumbs off his lap and placed them in his dish. "Suzie is very neat."

So what? Is that so great, to have "neat" as your leading attribute? Well, neat and pretty. With her shiny blond hair and bright blue eyes and pink lips, Suzie could be a commercial for soap. Mom is more interesting-looking. What's wrong with interesting? Does somebody have to be pretty to be desirable? Is that what Dad and Kevin think? The only good thing is to be pretty and neat?

"Mom is neat, too."

Dad smiled. "Smart, funny, ambitious, beautiful, yes. Neat, no."

"Funny?"

"Yeah." Dad looked like he was having a memory.

"What?"

"Nothing. Listen, Charlotte. I just want you to try. You know? Not be a lazy bum. You should hold yourself to a high standard, live a good life."

"Give me a break, please?"

"No," Dad said. "That is exactly the problem with . . . You let yourself off the hook of responsibility so darn easily. You are so glib, so impressed with yourself, but where is your moral fiber? Your core? Why are you so quick to excuse yourself from any responsibility? Why are you always looking for a break?"

Dad was right about me—I am lazy and glib, all that. But he's my father. He's supposed to think better of me than I do myself, isn't he? "It's just an expression," I mumbled.

"Even now. 'It's just, it's just.' It's an attitude. A lazy attitude."

My cell phone rang. I jumped, it startled me so much. I checked the caller ID: TESS. "I gotta take this." I stood up.

As I got to the door, Suzie appeared and asked sweetly, "Should I make some cocoa? ABC is taking a little more time to get a hold of himself."

I shrugged and pressed talk, passing her. "Hello?" I said, thinking, that's what I need, maybe—to take a little time to get a hold of myself.

"Hi," said Tess.

"Hi," I said. I tried to swallow past the ball in my throat.

"Well," she said.

"Well," I echoed. I didn't even know what to say to her, my best friend. If she still was. "How, um, was your Thanksgiving?"

"Fine." She sounded a little, maybe, snide. Snide would be so much better than hateful.

"Did you get my messages?" I asked her.

"Yes."

"Are you done being mad at me?"

"No," she said.

"Oh." I wasn't sure what I could do about that, so I said, "I miss you."

"Why didn't you tell me about your mother and Kevin's dad, you conniving witch?"

"I don't know," I said, relieved she was at least talking to me in sentence form. "I thought maybe it would go away."

"Like a zit?"

"No, like a, well, sort of, yes. If you don't touch it . . . yeah."

"Okay," she said. "I guess I get that."

"Thanks."

"Wow, huh?"

"I know," I said. "I'm sorry, Tess, really."

"I know."

"You forgive me?"

"You promise never to not tell me something again?"

"Yes," I said. "I promise."

"To tell me everything."

"Yes."

"Even if it's bad, or hard, or a zit."

"I'm getting a zit colony on my forehead," I told her.

"Who isn't?" she said, although she never has any.

"Otay," I said.

"Otay? Oh, otay. Oh, cutie. He still says that? I miss him. How is ABC?"

"Cute as ever," I said, all relieved and ready to tell her stories about how sweet the little guy was, all the adorable things he'd said that I'd been too tense to fully enjoy before this phone call. "This morning he was running naked through the . . ."

"I was thinking," Tess interrupted.

"Uh-oh."

"If they get married, Kevin will be your brother."

"Well, not . . ."

"And then if I marry Kevin, you and I will be sisters-in-law. Wouldn't that be so fun?"

Fun?

"Charlie?"

"That's a few jumps ahead," I managed to point out. "They're just . . . they're not . . ."

"Even so," Tess conceded. "How wild, if he's your brother and I come for a sleepover . . ."

"I don't think . . ." *Don't get in an argument with her,* I urged myself. I had just spent the whole week calling her, leaving notes in her locker, getting Jennifer to be a go-between—all to make her talk to me again. And now all I could think of saying to her was SHUT UP! "That would be pretty crazy," I made myself say instead.

"Do you think he would sneak into your room after midnight and . . ."

"Tess," I jumped in. "I, yes, that's, wow, we could really come up with a funny story out of that, but I don't want you to get your hopes up. That's a totally remote possibility. My mother and, and Mr. Lazarus—they are adults, adults with children to think about, and mortgages, and everything. They don't rush in to, it's not like, 'will you go out with me?' and then break up three days later . . ."

"It's a rental."

"What is?"

"Kevin's house," Tess said. "They rent it. So he doesn't have a mortgage."

*Breathe,* I told myself. She is talking to you again. "That wasn't my complete point, Tess."

149

"Whatever. Kevin thinks . . ." She stopped herself.

"Kevin thinks what?"

"He found a ring in his father's drawer."

No.

"You there?" she asked. "Charlie?"

"A what?"

"An engagement ring. He thinks his dad is going to ask your mom, soon."

"You're . . ." I tried to sit down on the edge of my bed, but I slid on the new flannel bathrobe Suzie had bought and laid out for me and fell on my butt on the floor. "Ow. No way. No way. Are you sure?"

"That's what Kevin said. We were at Brad's party."

"Party?"

"It was a last-minute thing Wednesday night, you were already at your dad's. It's not just that everybody was mad at you. You would've been invited, if you were here."

"Okay."

"It was lame, don't worry."

"Okay."

"Anyway, we went for a walk, me and Kevin, and we started kissing out up against the, you know, that shed in Brad's yard?"

"Tess."

"The—it's green, I think? Anyway, we were kissing and you know, whatever, and he touched my hair, and . . ."

"He touched your hair?"

"Yeah. Why?"

150

"Nothing. Which part, when he touched, what do you mean, he touched your hair?"

"Is that weird, you think? Maybe that is weird. He kind of twirled a piece of my hair around his finger. It was really kind of, intimate, sort of—he stopped kissing me and he was just, like, looking at my hair and twirling it."

"Huh."

"Yeah, maybe that's weird of him," she said. "I actually was starting to get all paranoid about if he was scouting for split ends, at the time, which is why I was like, what? And then he said, I found something in my father's drawer . . ."

"He told you that? While . . . while he was touching your hair?"

"Yes, he told me that, and he told me not to tell you, but, listen up, you piece of lint—you are my best friend, Charlie! I tell you everything. You get it? How about a little reciprocity, huh?"

"He . . . he . . . he thinks, he said . . ."

Suzie knocked on my door. "Cocoa's ready," she whispered. "Oh, Charlotte. Your socks, oops! Don't match." She winked.

I winked back. "Yes, they do." One was orange, the other black-and-red striped. They matched perfectly. "I'm on the phone," I added. She left then and I whispered into my phone, "Tell me exactly what Kevin said."

"You canNOT tell him you know. And you can definitely not tell your mother! It would ruin everything. Do you think she'll say yes?"

"I don't think . . . What did Kevin say exactly?" I asked. And then, unable to stop myself, asked, "He mentioned me?"

"Yeah," Tess said.

"While he was . . . What did he say?"

"He said you and he . . ."

"What?" I jumped up and started pacing. "He said he and I what?"

"Maybe I won't tell you," she said. "Maybe I'll keep it to myself, just as revenge."

"No!" I yelled. "No. Come on, Tess. Tell me what he said."

"Maybe sometime." I could almost hear her smiling.

"You stink."

"You love me," she said.

"Yes," I said. "You know I do."

"What's your mom doing this weekend?"

"Nothing," I said. "Catching up on work and stuff."

"Oh," Tess said.

"What?"

"Nothing."

"Why did you say 'oh' like that?" I asked her. "Come on, Tess. What? Do you know something about my mom that I don't know? Something else?"

# twenty-four

"HOW WAS YOUR Turkey Day?" I asked Mom in the car, driving home Sunday afternoon. No ring on her finger. It was the first thing I checked when she picked me up at Dad's.

"Fine," she said. "How was yours?"

"Fine," I said.

"Did Aunt Eileen and Uncle Moose come?"

"Yeah," I said. "All the usual suspects."

We drove along a while longer, listening to NPR. When the music finally came back on, replacing the talk, talk, talk, I asked, "Where did you spend the actual, you know, meal?"

She didn't answer right away, then asked, "What do you mean?"

"By what? Meal?"

She took a breath. "Why does this feel like the Inquisition?"

"I called you Thursday to say Happy Thanksgiving."

"No," Mom said. "I called you. Remember?"

"I had called earlier."

"But . . ."

"I didn't leave a message. Check caller ID if you don't believe me."

Mom turned down the music. "Let's take a step back, okay, baby?"

I looked out the window. Apparently Tess was right.

"Let's find a way to make this neutral," Mom said.

I didn't answer. What was there to say?

We listened to the music until it ended. When the guy came back on to talk about how much he had enjoyed the song he'd just played, Mom clicked the radio off.

"I went out with Joe," Mom said. "His ex-wife was in town over the weekend so she stayed with the kids."

"The kids," I muttered under my breath.

"She doesn't have a house here because she lives in Idaho. Apparently she's a masseuse, or in school to become a masseuse, I'm not sure."

"Whatever."

"Well, anyway, Joe wanted to give them time together, so he stayed in a hotel, and . . ."

"And you stayed with him."

"Actually," Mom said, "I stayed at home. As you know,

this is a very busy time of year for me, and I . . . you know what? That's not your business, Charlie."

I looked out the window at the bare trees, watching the lampposts zoom by backward. Mom drives fast, so we passed a lot of cars. I looked into each one, all those families sealed up separately in their cars, going home. I wondered what was going on with them—if their families were just fine or splitting apart, if they were happy all singing and bopping their heads like in one red Subaru, or if there were tensions and secrets even in that one.

I wondered for a few minutes what it would be like if I could tell Mom about Kevin and about Tess. When I used to be friends with Felicity, who is now a Pop-Tart, she used to tell her mother everything. We'd be playing together in Felicity's room and her mother would come in and actually play with us—dress up and be Drosselmeyer in our Nutcracker game, stuff like that. The first day Tess showed up at our school, in third grade, Felicity and I sat at their kitchen table with Felicity's mom and told her all about Tess—her long blond hair and light blue sweater and strong Southern accent, which, it turns out, was totally fake—and discussed whether or not we thought we'd like to be friends with her. Felicity's mom tucked her foot under her butt and chatted with us about it for an hour. When I got home that afternoon and told my mother a new kid came to school, she said, "That's nice. Do you have homework?"

At the time, I was a little disappointed. And maybe jealous.

But I guess because that's what I'm used to, it would feel seriously odd to tell my mother every detail of my life. *Mom, you know your boyfriend's son? Yeah, well, he's going out with my best friend, and he's actually the one I got caught kissing, and I'd kiss him again in a heartbeat.* I don't think so. I don't even like to tell myself that much.

*None of your business,* Mom said. It stung, hearing that, but at the same time, I would have to say I felt relieved. As much as I wanted to know everything, knowing everything about somebody else's secrets is kind of icky. And likewise with having to reveal all your own.

ABC had taught me, after he finished his time-out, his favorite song from preschool. Here's how it goes:

*Personal space,*
*Personal space,*
*Everybody needs some personal space,*
*Especially around their face.*

I took off my jacket and flipped on the seat warmer, humming ABC's song. I should send him a package, I decided, some candy and stickers. The seat warmer was fast: My butt was already starting to sweat. I didn't mind. Toast your buns, mom and I call it. It's what made us decide to buy this car—the toast-your-buns feature.

*Personal space, personal space . . .*

If she marries him, it occurred to me, I'd get demoted to the backseat. My personal space would be back there with two other kids and no toast-your-buns feature. Screw personal space and none of your business—I did the research on this car.

"Are you going to marry him?" I asked Mom, without turning to her.

"Oh, Charlie," she said. "I don't know. I like him. I love him. I really do. He's terrific. And even more important, I feel terrific when I'm with him. But I don't spend my time dreaming of wedding gowns and receptions, kiddo. I did that, I had that—I'm enjoying this time of my life more than I had expected to, which is great. That's all it's about for me right now."

I let that sit in the space between us. *Maybe that's what I need to do,* I thought. Maybe I need to just enjoy this time of my life as much as possible and not spend all this energy thinking about sistering Kevin or Mom marrying, or even whether or not I will ever kiss again. I could just enjoy the car ride home, being with Mom, and toasty buns on a gray Sunday afternoon.

"Otay," I said.

"Otay," Mom said.

We rode along thinking our own private thoughts until we hit the Boston traffic jam. The Mass Pike looked like a parking lot. So we put in Mom's Pat Benatar CD and sang along to "Hit Me with Your Best Shot" at the top of our voices.

We were that car, the car full of a family singing and bopping our heads around. And if the people in the other cars looked at us in horror or envy, well, let 'em.

# twenty-five

I WENT BACK to school feeling more on top of things. The time I'd spent at my father's was perhaps not ONLY horrible and boring and enlightening in terms of my continued shortcomings as a person with no athletic interests or good old American work ethic. Maybe, in addition to all that, it was helpful. Maybe it was actually an enforced time-out to get a hold of myself, like ABC.

I said hello to George and to Kevin with equally disinterested cheer. I even said hello to Felicity—or I think it was Felicity. It might have been one of her four or five best friends. It is hard to tell with them. But anyway I said hello nicely and got a very friendly hello and arm-touch in return.

I didn't hesitate in the doorway to bio, site of the original hair-twirl and falling feelings. Just sailed right in. No problem.

On Saturday, I went to the mall with Tess, Jennifer, and Darlene to shop for Christmas presents. We wandered from store to store, picking up some scented candles here, some CDs there, and red fuzzy gloves as a surprise for each of us, in big boxes with fancy bows on top. We decided we'd all open them up together that evening in Tess's sister's car on the way home. We kept saying stuff to one another like, "Come on, you guys, tell me what you got me" and "Don't tell Jennifer what we chose for her—she'll never guess!"

I was almost completely relaxed, just my regular self, out having regular fun with my regular friends, until we sat down to eat in the food court.

"Do you think I should buy something for Kevin?" Tess asked us.

I choked a little on a nacho chip.

"Isn't he Jewish?" Darlene asked, thumping me on the back.

"Yeah," Tess said. "But he could still get a present."

"True," said Jennifer. "I'm Hindu and you're buying me something."

"If you're lucky," I said. "What makes you think we are?" She stuck out her tongue at me. I stuck mine out, back.

"Are you buying him something?" Tess asked me.

"Me?" I casually shoved a whole handful of chips into my mouth.

"Well, your families are going to be together, right?"

I could feel my face getting hot. "We're going on the

twenty-sixth," I said. A few chips sputtered out as I talked. Very cool.

"Lovely," Tess said. "Do you think I should get him a CD?"

Jennifer groaned. We had just left the totally mobbed music store. "How about shoelaces?"

We all laughed. "Shoelaces? Shoelaces?"

"What?" asked Jennifer. "Boys like shoelaces. That's what I'm getting my brother. Hey, Charlie—maybe *you* should get him shoelaces."

I rolled my eyes and didn't buy him—or anybody in his family—anything.

# twenty-six

CHRISTMAS MORNING, Mom and I sat on the living room floor tearing open wrapping paper and eating candy from our stockings for breakfast. We are completely non-religious (well, actually Mom is antireligious; I am just apathetic) but, as Mom has always said, Santa doesn't mind. We each got a stack of books, some new socks (crazy colors for me, black for her) and long underwear, a new sweater, two CDs, a DVD and, to share, a new, really nice chess set. She also bought me a pair of Ugg shearling slip-on slippers, just like the ones she always wears. I put them on right away. "I love them," I said.

Mom kissed my head.

I wiggled my toes, digging them into the soft fuzz to begin wearing my own foot's shape into the slippers, just like

Mom's have worn into hers. In the past I've always gotten cheaper slippers, ordinary ones because my feet were still growing so fast, and Uggs are expensive, special. I splayed my legs out and lined them up with Mom's: four feet in a bobbling row, all in beautiful, ugly brown Uggs, all the same size.

"Thanks," I whispered.

After Mom opened the new deck of cards I'd chosen for her—she is a killer gin rummy player—she reached for her special present, the one with the silver bow. She gasped when she opened it and slipped it right onto her wrist. It was a spiral wire bracelet with lots of beads in tones of blue laced onto it. She kept touching it and glancing at it, I noticed. It cost a lot but I decided Dad and Suzie could wait for their gift, and Mom paid for the set of blocks I sent to ABC, so I really didn't have any other biggies to splurge on.

Mom was my one and only.

We put on some new music (it was not as good as I'd thought it would be when I put it on my wish list) and leaned back against the furniture. The great thing about Christmas Day is the lounging, I think. Candy for breakfast is second. Gifts are third. Though my Uggs were pretty special.

I was feeling really happy to be home instead of at Dad's, even despite the upcoming trip. That's for tomorrow, I decided; I'm not thinking about it today. At Dad's I would be dressed already (he can't stand to see people in their pajamas after dawn) and Suzie would have bagged up all the trash and vacuumed the room by now. I'd probably be hauling in firewood or shoveling the walk if I were there.

I picked up the cards I'd bought Mom. "Up for a challenge?" I asked. I have never beaten her at gin. She makes up new rules as we go along, I think. There's one thing she does when I have a good hand sometimes; she says, "I knock," and she knocks on the pile of cards and lays down her almost—but not quite—winning hand, and says she wins. How that works I still do not understand. But I was feeling generous.

Mom smiled. She put out her hand for the cards, but glanced at her watch on the way. A look of slight tension crossed her face.

"What?" I asked.

"What what?" she said.

"You look—are you going someplace?" In spite of myself I felt anger boiling up. She better not be going out. It's Christmas Day. I don't care if it has anything or nothing to do with religion—Christmas Day is Family Day, and I am her family.

"No," she said, but the tension lingered at the corners of her mouth. She opened the pack and slid the cards out. "I was just thinking maybe we should, after I slaughter you at gin, you know, clean up, get dressed, take a shower."

"After we get dressed?"

"What?" She started shuffling. She's great at that, too.

163

"Nothing. Why would we do that? It's Christmas Day. Let's stay gross all day. It's a . . ." I wanted to say *tradition*, but the word turned into a Ping-Pong ball and lodged in my throat.

She made a bridge out of the cards and they all fell together in a fluttering neat pile. Then she did it again, and again. She dealt the cards fast and sure, until we each had ten. It is a beautiful thing to watch, my mother with a deck of cards.

I didn't pick mine up until she did. As we sorted them out, she said, "Well, I just feel like a shower. In a little while."

"Is someone coming over later?" I asked quietly, calmly. Sort of like when my father is furious at me—that kind of whispering, with a warning in it.

"Do you want the card?" She pointed to the queen of hearts, lying in the discard pile.

"No."

"Yes," she said, sighing. "Joe and Kevin and Samantha are coming over around two. I invited them for cookies and to talk about the trip, and stuff. Pick a card."

I looked at the cards in my hand, in disarray. How could she do this to me? "I knock," I said, and dropped my cards in a heap on the floor.

By the time Kevin and family arrived, the living room was clean and so were we. I had put on my baggy old jeans and my dad's old Georgetown sweatshirt. Nothing new, nothing from her. Well, except my new Uggs.

Samantha had a card for each of us that she had made herself. Mine was a picture called "Chicken at Sunset" and it had a carefully drawn chicken in front of a blend of watercolors. I had to smile at the randomness. "Thanks," I said. "Did you know that I collect pictures of livestock at sunset?"

"Really?" she asked, and then I felt terrible. She looked so hopeful.

"She's kidding," Kevin said, putting his hand on her shoulder. "You have to get used to Charlie."

Samantha blushed. I felt myself do the same.

Mom came back with a tray of hot chocolates. At least she hadn't said "cocoa." I would have thrown up.

"Have some cookies," she said to the Lazarus family, which was bad enough. Mr. Lazarus took one, bit in, and said, "Mmm."

"They are Milanos," I felt I had to say. "You can buy a bag yourself if you want for, like, two and a half bucks."

He nodded at me. "Thanks for the tip," he said. Then he and my mother smiled dopily at each other for an unconscionably long time, until my mother came to her senses and turned away. "I have some little presents," she said. She handed a big box to Samantha and a small box to Kevin.

"Go ahead," Kevin said to his sister.

She unwrapped the paper without ripping it. Inside was a small pair of Uggs. Just like the ones on my own feet, the ones that were suddenly too hot, and not as special anymore.

"Thank you so much," Samantha said, and politely put them right on. She had no idea even what they were. And she's only eight—her feet are nowhere near done growing. I was ready for the Lazarus family to go away.

Kevin was opening his gift, but I didn't look up. I heard him say, "Thank you," and my mother explain that his father had told her he liked drawing, so these pencils were supposed to be special in some way. "They are," he said quietly. "Thanks. Really."

I didn't know Kevin liked to draw.

Mr. Lazarus reached into the bag beside him and pulled out a gift, which he handed to Mom. I was relieved to see it was not small enough to be a ring box. Mom tore open the wrapping. A bottle of olive oil was inside. She went over to Mr. Lazarus and, without a word, kissed him, then sat down beside him on the couch with his arm around her.

A box landed in my lap. I mumbled a thank-you and opened it. My stomach was in knots. It was the worst Christmas of my life. Inside the box was a pair of ski socks: one purple with yellow polka dots, one red-and-white striped.

I don't even know if I managed to say thanks. I was too caught up in wondering: Did Mom tell him I like mismatched socks, or had Kevin himself noticed another thing about me, besides that I am a good writer? And if he did, what did that mean?

# twenty-seven

SAMANTHA SAT BETWEEN me and Kevin in the back seat for the long ride up to Vermont. She asked if I wanted to play hangman. I told her I got carsick. She said she was sorry to hear that, and took *The Hobbit* out of her backpack, which she read from beginning to end, while twirling a strand of her own hair. I guess hair-twirling runs in their family. Kevin drummed on his leg and listened to music through his earphones. There was no singing in the car this time around, no personal space. I looked out my window the whole time, mourning my untoasted buns.

The house was fine but upside down, with the bedrooms downstairs and the living room and kitchen upstairs. There was a pool table behind the couch and a fireplace in front of it. It looked like an L.L. Bean ad. Kevin and his father got the twin beds in the red room, Samantha and I each got a twin bed in the yellow room and my mother was marooned on her own in the big blue room with its one king-sized bed.

The first night, after we hauled all our stuff in and unpacked it and ate the dinner Mr. Lazarus cooked for us—pasta à la vodka, which tasted a lot better than it looked, which isn't saying much—I went downstairs and took my shower. I brought my pajamas and a sweatshirt into the bathroom with me. I didn't need to go parading around as if we were all actually related. Everybody was being perfectly pleasant and I didn't want to be the pouty brat of the group, but no way was I going to pretend we were suddenly the Brady Bunch either.

After I was all dried off and dressed, I dashed across the hall to the yellow room and slipped under my covers. I got out my book and read for a while, but I guess I was pretty wiped out because I was asleep before anybody else came down.

When I woke up the next morning, Samantha was fast asleep in the bed across the room. Her hands were in prayer position, tucked under her cheek. She looked so sweet and innocent. I lay there imagining how it would be if she actually became my sister, my half sister, the first in line to be my maid of honor at my wedding, bumping out Tess. Would she come to me asking my advice about school (probably not) or boys (yikes) as she got older? Would she look up to me? Would I protect her and, like, brush her hair for her?

It was too weird. I got up quickly and dashed to the bathroom to brush my teeth, thinking, this is a good plan, doing all my personal stuff before anybody else. I could just be in a different time zone and not have nearly as much stress, even if we all have to live together.

I thought about peeking into one of the other bedrooms to check that the sleeping arrangements were as advertised, but decided the embarrassment potential outweighed the nosiness factor by a heck of a lot. So instead I headed up the stairs to make myself some breakfast, humming *personal space, personal space,* and almost jumped out of my skin when Mr. Lazarus said, "Hi, Charlie!"

He was standing at the counter holding a mug in one hand and a newspaper in the other, wearing his long underwear.

"Hi."

I went past him to the fridge and took out the milk. As I was pouring myself a big glass, he asked, "Psyched to ski?"

I nodded. "So is your wife really a fighter pilot or a masseuse?"

"She was in the Air Force," he said. "Briefly. Now she's a masseuse. Ex-wife."

"And you're a photojournalist?"

"Photographer." He nodded some more.

"What kind of photographs do you take?" I hated myself. I would not, I knew, have been doing this if anybody else had been in the room. He obviously didn't know me well

169

enough to have planned for security. "Abstracts? Nudes? Have you had, like, shows of your work in galleries?"

"I do weddings," he said, leaning back against the counter and crossing his legs. "Bar mitzvahs, holiday cards. That kind of thing."

"Oh," I said. Of course, I already knew that.

"But your intuition is right, your jab."

"I wasn't . . ."

"Come on," he said. "Of course you were. Don't back off. I like you better when you let your talons show."

"My what?" I was starting to regret picking on him. He had seemed as meek and pitiable as a substitute teacher. Suddenly I wasn't so sure.

"Yes," he said, almost drawling. "I did want to be the kind of photographer who showed in galleries. That was my ambition."

"Sorry," I said.

"But I love what I do now."

"That's nice," I said.

"Yes it is," he answered. "You know why?"

"Why it's nice?"

"Why I like it. Because my job is to see the beauty in people, and then show it."

"What if they're ugly?"

"Then I'm not looking well enough," he answered. "Because we are all amazingly, shockingly beautiful. Aren't we?"

"You must know different people than I do," I said.

He smiled. "What's yours?"

"My what?"

"Your ambition." He sipped from his mug.

"To get out of this conversation?"

He laughed. He has a really generous laugh. I could not entirely blame my mother for liking this guy, despite my ambition to. I shrugged, trying not to smile myself in response, and said, "I don't know."

"Sure you do."

"I'm only fourteen."

"I know how old you are." When he smiles his canine teeth are noticeable. It gives him a sort of vampire look, or maybe it was just that he looked a lot like Kevin, who had been a vampire for Halloween. Or maybe I was just panicking.

"I honestly have very little ambition."

"Your mother was right," he said.

"My mother told you I have very little ambition?"

"She said that you're like her, but more so."

I stood at the top of the bunny slope praying *don't fall, don't fall* and waiting for my turn with all the other kids whose parents had abandoned them to ski-school jail. Samantha went first of the three of us. She did fine, slow and cautious, nice wide turns. She got sent to a group of kids who looked about her size.

*A higher group*, I prayed. If I'm with his little sister and he's doing black diamonds, I will fake a broken leg and sit in the lodge. My ambition, Mr. Lazarus wanted to know? To not make a fool of myself in front of your son. That's all. Forget Pulitzers, Nobels, canonizations, even falling indescribably madly passionately out of control in love. I just want to *not fall*. At all. In anything. That is the entirety of my ambition.

Kevin went next. He did tight little turns, his boots locked together. Highest group. Great. Just great.

I was next. I clamped my knees against each other and leaned forward. I was going so slow I thought I might start moving uphill. But I eventually made my way down and was relieved and surprised when the head ski guy pointed his pole directly at Kevin.

Success.

I duck-walked up to him and the beautiful redhead ski instructor beside him. There was nobody else in the group yet. I was so relieved I gave the instructor an uncharacteristically cheerful hello.

"Hi," she said. "I'm Helena, and this guy is Kevin."

"I know," I said. I just achieved my life's ambition. I'm done now. I can totally relax and coast for the rest of my life.

"Oh." Helena looked back and forth between us. "Are you guys . . ."

"Cousins," Kevin said.

"Oh, great, so you've probably skied together a lot. No

inside jokes, now, promise?" Helena stretched over her skis. "So what's your name?" she asked me.

"We call her Chuck," Kevin said.

"Chuck?"

"Short for Charlotte," I said.

"I love that," Helena said.

"Me, too," I mumbled.

Helena skied over to her boss to see if any other kids were getting assigned to her.

"Ready, Chuck?" Kevin shot me a sly smirk.

Some of my other ambitions came charging back.

# twenty-eight

WHEN I HEARD footsteps coming toward the bedroom that night, I faked sleep.

"Good night," Kevin whispered.

"Hey," Samantha said, near my head. "I won."

"You cheated."

"You can't cheat in chess. You promised."

"Ugh. Fine." I heard Kevin tiptoe loudly into the room.

I opened the eye that was against the pillow. Kevin had his back to me, and Samantha's eyes were closed. This is exactly what Kevin did:

He poked her on the forehead and said, "North."

He poked her chin and said, "South."

He poked her left cheek and said, "East."

He poked her right cheek and said, "West."

Then he turned to go.

"Kevin!" she said.

"Come on, Samantha. Enough."

"That was not a whole Global Kiss," she said.

He groaned.

"I would've given you the whole five dollars if you had won," she said.

Kevin came back into the room. He kissed the top of her head and grumbled, "I love you all over the map."

Her eyes were closed. "Thanks," she whispered. "Do you miss her, too?"

"No," Kevin said.

"I do." Samantha opened her eyes.

"Good night," Kevin said, and left the room, closing the door gently on his way.

I closed my eyes quickly. I listened as Samantha got into her pajamas and then into her bed. When I opened my eyes, she was reading with a flashlight. At that moment she glanced over at me. We both gasped a little, both caught.

"Were you awake the whole time?"

I paused a second too long, trying to formulate a lie.

"I thought so," she said. "Did you see the Global Kiss?"

"The what?"

"Global Kiss—north, south . . ."

"Yeah," I said. "Global Kiss, huh?"

Samantha nodded. "My mother made it up for Kevin when he was little, and since she's, you know, away, he gives it to me sometimes. Isn't it nice?"

"Yes," I said.

"My dad loves your mom," she whispered. "I think."

"I think so, too," I whispered back.

"Do you love Kevin?"

"Why . . . why . . . why do you ask?" I very casually responded.

"You and he get that same blotchy look around each other that our parents get."

"Really?" I asked, feeling somewhat blotchy suddenly. "He does? Kevin does? Or is it just me, getting blotchy?"

"No," she said, bless her. "Him, too."

"He's going out with my best friend."

"I know," she whispered.

We raised our eyebrows at each other, across the yellow carpet. She got it, she knew, she was on my side. So I asked her: "What do you think I should do?"

"I don't know," she whispered. "I'm only eight. Do you mind if I read some more now?"

"Sure," I said, and rolled over. I don't think I fell asleep for hours.

# twenty-nine

I TRIED TO convince myself not to like him. I really did. I was getting to know him a lot better. Sometimes his nose was a little runny, a particularly unattractive quality despite suffering from it—on occasion—myself. His lips were slightly chapped, which made him look marginally less kissable. And when I said, "What if Helena's boyfriend wanted to marry her, but his last name was Handbasket?" Kevin didn't get it, or at least didn't die laughing.

How could I be crazy about somebody like that? Also, he ate French fries with mustard and hummed while he skied (okay, that was pretty cute). Oh, and as we were waiting in the lift line on the second day, he told me, "Your socks don't match." I was about to explain to him that mismatched socks was my thing, the special thing about me, my style, when I realized, okay, obviously it was my mother who had told Mr. Lazarus about the socks for the gift. It wasn't Kevin. He had never noticed. I shrugged and turned away from him, pretending to concentrate on the chair approaching us from behind.

But then, once the safety bar was down and we were floating silently up the mountain, he leaned against me, slightly. His jacket pressed against mine, and I stopped caring about anything else.

We skied hard and fast, following Helena in a line down the mountian, all in the same rhythm. It was great. The third day we decided to avoid the lunch crush by waiting until two to eat. My stomach wasn't just growling, it was roaring. We each got a tray and met back at the table where we'd left our hats and mittens, and wolfed down our food without talking. I only looked up when I heard Kevin slurping the dregs of his soda. He'd gotten a small. I smirked at him as I casually sipped from my jumbo.

"Oh, yeah?" he asked, and plopped his straw into my cup, too.

I started to open my mouth to protest the gall of that and the germs (oh, whoa, his germs, again) but he was chugging all my soda so I started sipping as fast as I could. We were so close our noses were practically touching. We sucked my cup dry in about five seconds flat.

"Thanks," he whispered, his lips still around his straw.

"Uh-huh," I breathed. Then, pretending I had to tighten my boot buckle, I ducked under the table. As I sat up I slammed my head on the underside and fell off my chair onto the floor.

"One wipeout for Chuck," Helena cheered. "Come on, let's ski."

My legs were slightly shaky on the next few runs, probably from skiing so hard. Right. Just before four o'clock, racing down so we could get one last run in, I was between Helena and Kevin. We were coming down Revenge, our favorite trail. It was the time of day when the shadows can really mess you up, camouflage the moguls just as your legs are starting to feel like overcooked spaghetti, but I was keeping up with Helena, in a good crouch, feeling good and free. She skidded to a stop and I edged in, just above her. I was breathing a little hard, but I'd gotten over being embarrassed about that and trying to hide it from her. She smiled at me. "You and your cousin are really improving this . . ."

She stopped and looked up the hill. I turned to see what she was looking at and saw Kevin's jacket, smashing me in the face.

When we stopped tumbling and lay still, I first felt only cold on my neck. Then I felt a weight on top of me and something soft on my cheek. It took me a second to realize it was Kevin's cheek.

He wasn't moving.

"Hey," I said softly.

I felt him shift. Phew.

"You okay, Chuck?" he asked.

"I don't know," I said. "I guess so. I'm looking at the

clouds. Maybe I'm dead."

He lifted his head off mine. Snow crusted the bits of hair that stuck out of his hat, and his eyebrows, and his mouth.

"Nice stop, Santa," I told him.

He sniffed. "You like that? Been working on that all week. To impress you."

"Oh," I said. "You sure did. Swept me off my feet."

Luckily Helena pulled him off me then, and we got caught up in the tumult of finding our scattered skis and poles and assuring her that neither one of us had to be taken down in the stretcher. We skied down in tandem, racing but not full-out. The sun was heading down and everything looked glazed, including us. And the smell of hamburgers from the lodge was making me weak with hunger.

"Let's call it a day, huh?" Helena suggested when we got to the bottom.

I thought of six wiseguy suggestions of what we should call it instead of a day, but managed to hold them in. Instead I bumped my shoulder into Kevin, who toppled over.

"Oh, Chuck, now you're asking for it," he yelled from the ground.

I jumped out of my skis and almost got away before he attacked me with a handful of snow in my face.

It was freezing.

It was great.

It was the beginning.

# thirty

I WATCHED FROM behind my book as Kevin and his father played pool. Mom shuffled her cards and asked if anybody wanted to play gin. Samantha tried seven-card (which Mom hates and never lets me play even when I was Samantha's age—*you're not a baby; hold ten cards, come on!*) but even with only seven, Samantha kept dropping them. They laughed a lot, the two of them, and eventually gave up. I was tempted to give in and play with Mom too, but then I looked over at Samantha's little Ugg slippers. I settled back into my book. Mom wasn't getting off that easy, even if I was having a decent time after all on this dumb trip she planned.

Okay, better than decent.

It was hard for me to pull down my smile.

"Are you guys enjoying ski school?" Mr. Lazarus asked.

"It's okay," Samantha said.

"Yeah," said Kevin, and smirked at me. "It's okay. Right?"

Maybe it wasn't a slow sexy smile like he was happy to see me and I looked good, but it was a smile, more than a smile, a smirk, and anyway it was just for me. Like he knew me, like he could see what I was thinking, like—like he liked me. Me.

I kept looking at his lips. I couldn't help myself.

*Will I kiss him?* I couldn't stop thinking that. I want to kiss him. *Will we kiss?* I kissed him once before; maybe it's like a prior thing, a continuation, so it wouldn't count as anything. Maybe it would be a big nothing. So why couldn't I stop thinking, *what will happen if we kiss?*

"Eight ball in the corner pocket," Kevin said, and sank it clean.

"Phew," said Mr. Lazarus. "You whooped me." He plopped down beside my mother.

Kevin leaned on the pool table. "Who's next?"

I stood up. "Me."

"Great," he said.

I can't believe I could even hit the cue ball, never mind clonk the other balls with it. But I saw that Kevin's hands were shaking a little when he broke, and for some reason that calmed me down. I felt really good, even when I noticed he was watching me. Especially, in fact, noticing that. I mean, there I was, with my hat head, in big floppy sweatpants and my dad's old black turtleneck and thick cozy socks—so far from pretty, and yet, I did not feel embarrassed. I did not feel ugly or even unattractive.

I felt sexy.

And I liked feeling that way.

Not just sexy—I felt, and there it was again, the same feeling as when I first flirted with him: powerful.

And I guess I was, because I won.

I was more surprised than anybody. I mean, Kevin has a pool table in his house at home, and I am a total klutz. But I think he was distracted, and I think it was me who was distracting him. Could anything be more exciting than that?

All those romantic ideas I had about falling in love were very sweet and pastel compared to how this felt.

I did a little bit of taunting him—you know, of the "you're going down, loser" variety, especially after I knocked in the eight ball on my first try. "Yes!" I shouted, arms up. I wasn't even trying to hold down my smile anymore.

"Now what?" he asked.

I shrugged. Yes, good question: Now what?

We stood there for a while. I had so much adrenaline rushing through me I could have done a triathlon, won one. That word twisted my stomach momentarily, and I headed toward the other half of the living room to sit, to calm myself down, to get a hold of myself. Personal space.

Samantha was lying on the floor on her back with a book held up in the air above her. My mother and Mr. Lazarus were on the big couch, her feet in his lap, him massaging them. The only places left to sit were the wood chair or the smaller couch.

I picked the couch.

So did Kevin.

So much for personal space or calming myself down. I sat upright and tapped my feet against the floor. I was having trouble staying rooted to the couch. It was entirely possible I could spin up to the ceiling if I didn't grip the couch cushion. Kevin was drumming on his knees, rocking a bit. I reached for the bowl of pistachio nuts. I guess he thought that seemed like a good idea because he copied.

We sat there like that for what felt like a pretty long time, the only sounds the crackling of the fire, and the cracking of pistachio nutshells. My breath, his breath, shells into the small glass bowl on the table. When one log fell off another in the fireplace, Kevin and I both jumped.

Mr. Lazarus stood up to rearrange the logs. It was sort of a pathetic fire. He took the last log from what had been a big pile when we arrived and flung it on top, then poked it a few times. I am not an expert at making fires but this did not seem to be the most effective technique. Nobody said anything for a minute.

"Maybe we need more kindling," Mr. Lazarus said.

"And some more wood, more logs," Mom suggested.

"Yeah." Mr. Lazarus put his hands on his hips and watched the wisps of flame. "Guess I'll go out and get some more—I think the firewood is stacked somewhere in the back. I wish it weren't so cold."

"I'll get it," Kevin volunteered, popping up.

"I'll help," I added, standing, too.

"Really?" Mom tilted her head at me.

"No problem," I said. "I like the cold."

"You do?"

I was already heading downstairs so I didn't answer. Luckily she was preoccupied with Mr. Lazarus and not wanting to budge from the couch, or she surely would have followed me down to follow up, since I have always actually been a complete baby about the cold. But it turns out I'm more complex than any of us knew.

Without a word, Kevin and I stomped into our boots and pulled on jackets, hats, mittens. He yanked open the heavy front door and I followed him out into the cold. It was wicked cold, too. We breathed smoke, like dragons.

We walked around the house past the car. There was a wooden fence blocking the way and no wood pile anywhere. "Hmm," he said, and I cracked up. Somehow that just seemed cataclysmically funny, that "Hmm" with his fists on his hips and his legs all scrawny-looking in just their long underwear hanging down below his bulky jacket. I don't know. Maybe I was tense. I could barely stand, I was so hysterical.

He laughed, too, a little at first, then more. When it was slightly dying down, he took a breath, and I thought he was going to do just what Tess would have done, which is to say

"Hmm" again and get me all doubled over fresh. But instead what he did was, he put his hand on my back and said, "Let's try the other way."

As we passed the car again, and the front door, his hand stayed on my back, which meant his arm was kind of guiding me. I let myself press back slightly against it and noticed my laughing was gone. My whole body was hot and cold at the same time. We came to a huge pile of logs and stopped in front of it, but he didn't start collecting any.

His hand stayed where it was and he turned to look at me. His face was pretty close to mine and he whispered, "So. Chuck . . ."

"So," I answered.

"What if . . ."

My heart pounded even harder. "What if what?"

He swallowed, looked at a spot on my jacket, then lifted his other arm and put his mitten on the sleeve of my jacket. "What would you do if I kissed you?"

I waited. For once I couldn't talk.

He lifted his eyes to mine but otherwise didn't move. "You and me," he whispered. "What if we just . . ."

"We can't."

"Do you want to?"

Did I want to. "Do you?" I asked.

"Yeah." He moved, tilted, slightly closer to me. "I do. Do you?"

"Yeah," I admitted. I could feel myself shaking. "But . . ."

"Yeah," he breathed.

*I should stop this,* I thought. *I should smile or joke or say we shouldn't.* His eyes were so blue. I looked down at his mouth and whispered, "But we shouldn't."

"Okay," he said, backing the tiniest bit away. Just enough so I couldn't feel the warmth of his breath anymore.

"But . . ." I said.

"But you want to," he said.

I nodded, and my eyes went back up to his.

"And I want to."

"But if we do . . ." I whispered. "If we kiss . . ."

"Yeah."

His face neared mine again. His blue, blue eyes closed. *Oh no,* I thought as lightly, softly, his lips touched mine.

# thirty-one

WOW.

So.

We kissed. We kissed for a minute; then we stopped, looked at each other, and kissed a few little kisses, then another big deep kiss again, his arms holding me tight and mine on his back, too. It was not at all disgusting this time. My fingers were sweating in my mittens but my legs were icy and I was shaking, shivering, freezing, melting, cold, hot.

"You're shivering," he whispered.

I sniffled. "Yeah."

His kissed me lightly again, on the lips. "You want to go in?"

"No," I said.

He laughed a one-exhale laugh and kissed me again. Our

lips were soft together. It occurred to me that maybe I'd like French toast now, too.

My teeth were chattering, hard and loud. "I guess we should go in."

"They'll be wondering," he said, as we headed back, then stopped short. "Wood. We ought to bring some wood."

"Good plan," I said. "Less obvious."

We bent and got armloads. I was shivering so much I dropped a few. As we got to the door and Kevin leaned against it, trying to get to the doorknob, I was thinking, this is too weird. How can we go back in there now? How do I act toward him in front of everybody?

"What am I going to do with you?" I whispered.

The door swung open. He raised his eyebrows and whispered back, "Anything you want."

Well, try being normal after a comment like that. I was shaking so much by the time we got upstairs I just dumped my whole pile of wood on the floor and ignored all the chatter about what took you so long and we were about to send out the sled dogs to find you, and, dreading that Mom might mention the figurative cow from the last time I kissed Kevin, I announced that I was chilled and going to take a shower.

I took a long hot one. The shivering eased but didn't stop, especially when I started thinking, what do I do if he's there when I open the bathroom door? I dried off, got into my flannel pajamas, brushed my teeth, and combed my hair. In the mirror I looked flushed and good, better than usual. Maybe better even than Tess.

Tess.

I opened the door slowly and looked around. Nobody there. I tiptoed across the hall and slipped into my bed. I lay there thinking about what Tess had said about if my mother married Kevin's father and she slept over and Kevin snuck into my room, and thought, what if he sneaks in tonight? It would be to be with me. *I am the worst friend,* I thought. What am I going to do? He kissed me, oh boy, did he kiss me, and I want to kiss him again, more. When can I kiss him again? Tomorrow on the ski lift? I will never be able to sleep for all these thoughts and desires and the excitement and feeling of the kissing—and the next thing I knew I was waking up and it was morning.

My mother was on the edge of my bed with her hand on my forehead. "You're sick," she said, and for a minute I thought she had found out.

"Why?"

"Why? I don't know. You have a fever. It's eleven o'clock. When I tried to wake you to ski, at eight, you were sort of delirious."

"I was?" Just what I needed. "Why? What did I say?"

"Nonsense. Tess, mostly. I think you thought I was Tess. You were really upset and incoherent, and then apologizing a lot. It was very sweet. She called this morning, by the way, about an hour ago, to say Happy New Year's Eve."

"Tess did?"

"Yeah," said Mom.

I closed my eyes. They burned. "Did Kevin talk to her?"

"He was long gone. Joe took him and Samantha to ski. Just us, today. I brought you some Motrin."

She helped me upstairs and tucked a blanket around me. I felt like crap, especially anytime I moved. Mom put on some soft classical music and I guess I dozed, on and off. It was kind of nice. She puttered around, taking care of me. She put a cotton T-shirt of hers under my face, in case the throw pillow was a little scratchy, and made me some weak tea. A little later she brought me some saltines on a plate and some ginger ale, and all that attention made me feel so much better that I said, "Want to play gin?"

She won, of course, but without knocking.

"He's nice," I said, sinking down into the couch again. I was feeling dizzy but generous.

"Joe?" Mom asked.

"Yeah. A little intense, but I guess nice."

"He really is." Mom shuffled the cards.

"And you seem, kind of, happy. Around him."

"Thanks. Yeah, I feel happy. Giddy, sometimes, but mostly just happy."

"Is that—did you ever feel like that around Daddy?"

Mom smiled. "No. I felt . . . How did I feel? You really want to know?"

"Yes," I said, realizing I really did.

"Passionate," she said. "I felt, oh, I felt off-balance,

vulnerable, nervous . . . I think I had anxiety confused with love."

"Really?" *You mean they're separate?*

"I know that sounds ridiculous," she said. "But I was young. Phew. I hope you're never that kind of young."

Yeah, I wished I weren't too. Unfortunately, I knew exactly what she meant. Or maybe I didn't. With me and Kevin, it's deeper than just anxiety. It's powerful. It's so intense. *It has to be love,* I thought. It's different. It's the kind of love that burns down the world. Maybe.

"With your dad, and I don't want to, maybe I shouldn't tell you this. He's your father . . ."

"That's okay," I said, sitting up a little. "I want you to."

"I just, I don't want you to think I am comparing him and Joe."

"I don't even really remember you guys together, so . . ."

"My heart used to race every time I saw him. Your father. And we were together for five years, but it never died down." She thumped her closed fist against her chest, *thump, thump, thump.* "My heart would be clanging against my ribs, just at the sight of his face, his profile. Even when we were fighting, hating, even all through the divorce—it was always really intense between us. I can't explain it."

"It's indescribable," I said.

"Yeah." She shook her head. "And I thought that meant it was true love. But it wasn't, not really. It was—I don't know how else to say this—lust. A chemical reaction. Lust and anxiety. But it wasn't, oh Charlie, we love each other now, your dad and I, in a way, in a deeper way. I love him for giving me you. And there's a part of me, of my heart, that I suppose will always belong to him. But we were never right for each other. He never got my jokes, you know? He never understood my passions or why the things that mattered to me really did matter to me. And, to be fair, I never really fathomed him, either."

"You, whatever, fathom *him*, though? Joe?"

She nodded. "I do. I feel like myself with him, like all the different parts of myself, my best, my strongest self. In the beginning I worried it wasn't love, it couldn't be, because my heart wasn't pounding all the time, I wasn't scared he might grab it out of my chest and stomp on it. Isn't that stupid?"

I shrugged. The possibility of having my heart stomped on when we got back home to reality was, in my medical opinion, largely responsible for my current fever. "Pretty stupid," I said.

"I got over that when I realized how good I felt every time I was with Joe. He really listens to me, thinks about what I've said, makes me think . . ."

I nodded. That was nice but maybe I didn't want to know any more about how in love my mother felt. I closed my eyes and she stopped talking. I thought about Helena Handbasket and whether Kevin fathoms me. Uh, well, no, probably not. I just, I really like the way my insides feel when he stands near me. Does that mean it might only be chemical?

I guess I dozed off again because the next thing I knew the Lazarus family was back, building another fire and clattering around, talking about how icy the conditions were and how I hadn't missed a thing. Three new kids were added to our class, Kevin mentioned, without looking at me directly. He said they were okay, good skiers, it was fun. He said they went down some new black diamonds, really fast, and one kid named Annie was awesome on the bumps. Annie? I hated her. Stupid show-off jerk.

Mr. Lazarus asked if I was feeling better. I was, a tiny bit, but I was in a pout by then so I shrugged. He said, "I better cancel our reservation for tonight."

"Why don't you guys go out?" Mom suggested. "Charlie and I will ring in the New Year on the couch."

"No," he said. "That's silly. We'll all stay in. That's fine. I saw a fondue set in the closet. Maybe I'll do a run up to the store and . . ."

"No," I said from the couch. "I'm not ruining everybody's night. I don't need you all crowding me anyway. Go."

"Yeah," said Kevin.

*Yeah?* I thought. *Yeah?* He's that desperate to get away from me? How nice, when I'm suffering with a fever and who knows what's wrong with me? YEAH? Why is it every time I kiss him he turns on me? That's it, I am done kissing. This fever is a sign.

But then Kevin said, "Why don't you guys go out? We'll stay here. We'll have a better time if we don't have to sit at a long drawn-out dinner at some boring restaurant."

He wanted to stay home alone with me? What did that mean? I wasn't sure I could handle it. Four minutes alone by the wood pile and I was spiking fevers to 103. A whole night? Alone together? I'd end up in the hospital for sure.

He wanted to be with me. He was sending everybody else away.

"What about me?" Samantha asked.

"You'll help me take care of Charlie," Kevin told her.

Oh.

"Okay," said Samantha.

I wasn't sure if I felt relieved or disappointed, but everybody else looked happy with the plan. So that's what happened, except that I don't know how much care they took of me.

I was drifting in and out of sleep. I woke up a few times and they were watching TV, or shooting pool, or eating something that smelled nauseatingly of onions. My fever was back, clearly, but I didn't want to ask for Motrin when they should've been taking care of me, or my mother should've. I was feeling totally sorry for myself but then that sort of flipped and I decided I deserved to feel this bad, worse, for what I'd done. I kissed my best friend's boyfriend, more than kissed him—really, deeply, passionately kissed him.

And liked it.

And wanted to do it again.

There was no denying what we had done this time; no

going back. There was something between us now and we were going to have to deal with it.

What did I want? To sneak out in the cold and kiss whenever possible? There's something incredibly electrifying about that, I had to admit. I wanted Samantha to fall asleep and him to lie down next to me on the couch, and kiss me as we listened for the crunch of car tires on the snow outside. But what about when we got home? Back to Tess? How would it feel to see him walk down the hall in school with her, holding hands, as they had started to do just before vacation? What then? Would he walk me home and kiss me in the woods afterward? How sustainable is that?

Not.

I didn't want to cat around behind her back, behind everybody's back, kiss him and then talk on the phone with her about him and how things are going between them.

I wanted him to dump her, my beautiful, confident best friend who was in love with him, and choose me, ask me out, fall in love with me. Me. I wanted him to think I was the pretty one, smarter, funnier, more fun, sexier, deeper, better. Tell me he loves me, tell the world he loves me. Make the grand gesture.

Maybe.

Or maybe I wanted to go back to just enjoying wondering what it would feel like if we kissed again. Anticipating, fantasizing—that was fun, and innocent.

Or maybe I wanted to go back even further, to no

interest in kissing, to the day he asked if I had studied for the bio quiz and I could say, "Yup, a little" and just walk into class. Back before lust.

But on it goes. Tick, tock, almost next year, and I couldn't even make a resolution to be more innocent. Too late. I had changed. I was different now.

I was not a good girl anymore, if I ever had been.

I could feel myself heating up and getting muddled. I drifted back to sleep for a while, I think, because I had weird dreams of kissing and fighting and wind, and I think I was in a train station at one point. I jolted awake and didn't know where anybody was. I was all alone. I suddenly really needed to be in a bed so I dragged myself downstairs trailing the blanket behind me like a little kid, a sad little lonely pathetic kid.

# thirty-two

THEY GOT ENGAGED.

My mother was going to marry Kevin's father. My head was so messed up my eyes were crossing. Literally. I had to keep pressing my palms against them to keep them from spinning.

Mom woke me up in the morning to tell me and show me the ring. It was beautiful, a sapphire with a small diamond on either side. It looked perfect on her hand. We went to her big bed and she told me all about how he'd asked, flowers, tears, down on one knee, until I really couldn't take it anymore. I headed upstairs to get myself some crackers, or privacy.

Mr. Lazarus cut me off at the stairs and asked to speak with me alone. "Sure," I said, because, truly, what more could happen? I was a long way from the girl who'd cried in Mr. Hair-Man's office over my mother being called when I'd kissed Kevin. The first time. Holy crap.

I grabbed my jacket off the hook and stomped into my boots.

"I want to ask for your blessing," Mr. Lazarus told me as we walked outside, toward the wood pile of all places.

"My blessing?" It was a bit hard for me to concentrate there. Scene of the crime, so to speak.

"To marry your mother. I love her, Charlie. I love her very much."

"I know." I wrapped my arms around myself the way Kevin had wrapped his around me in an earlier lifetime, in that same spot.

"I know there are some parts of this that are awkward . . ."

He should only know. "Yeah."

"You and Kevin are . . ."

"Are what?" *Does he know?* "We're friends," I snapped, sounding a heck of a lot more defensive than I'd planned to.

"What?" he asked. "Yes, right. You guys are having some fun this week, right?"

Shoot me now. "Depends what you mean, I suppose."

"What I mean is, you and Kevin are clearly old enough to, well, feel . . . a little . . . awkward, blending families at this stage."

"Uh-huh," I said. Samantha knew; obviously Joe knew. Did my mother, too? Was she inside interrogating Kevin at this moment? Would he admit or deny? We should have made a plan. Tess would've made a plan. Tess.

"You seem very tense."

"I'm not!"

He smiled Kevin's smile. Okay, that denial sounded completely tense, even I had to admit, and I am clearly a champion of denial.

"Well," I said. "This is a slightly tense situation."

"Yes, I know that it is, Charlie . . . but . . ."

"What?" *Let's cut to the chase, here. I'm getting frostbite. How long does it take to say don't kiss him ever again?*

"I think we could make a really great family. I will never try to be your father or to come between you and your dad in any way."

"Okay." So, did he not know then? Was this a case of ABC's theory that you can't know what I'm thinking because you're not me? I'm sorry—my dad? He thought I was tense because of my *dad*?

"I think you and I could have some fun together, Charlie. I'm going to try to be a really good stepfather to you. I like you so much already, your tough façade, your killer instincts, your independence, your vulnerability. I want to really get to know you even better—what makes you tick, what your hopes and dreams are. Okay?"

"Sure, Mr. Lazarus," I said. Because, truly, what else could I say? And I was cold. Independence? Please. And if he didn't already know my hopes or dreams, I was perfectly happy to keep it that way. Nobody ever needed to know. Good lord. Tess.

He put his mittens on my jacket sleeves, which kind of freaked me out, as an echo of the last time I'd stood there with someone's mittens on my sleeves. "Will you please call me Joe?"

"Maybe someday," I said. "Can we go in? I have to make a phone call."

She picked up on the third ring. My stomach was in knots as soon as I heard her voice. I sat down on the floor. "Tess?"

"Hey, pal," she said. "I heard you were sick. Are you better? Happy New Year."

Kevin walked over, his cereal bowl in hand. "Who's that?" he whispered.

"Tess," I said. If she had heard I was sick it meant he'd called her already, right? What had he told her?

"Yeah," she said. "You okay? You don't sound good. What's wrong with you?"

What's wrong with me? Now there's a question.

"I . . ." My breakfast was gurgling around inside my stomach. "What did . . ." I looked at Kevin and mouthed, *did you tell her?*

He shook his head.

"Charlie? What's going on there?"

"You were right, Tess," I said in a rush, looking at Kevin. "He gave her a ring. They're getting married."

"Oh, my God! Charlie! Charlie?"

"Yeah."

Kevin stepped toward me. "Chuck . . ." The room tilted.

"Tess, I have to . . ." I dropped the phone on Kevin's foot, ran to the bathroom, and puked my guts up.

# thirty-three

KEVIN AND I didn't talk about what had happened or what we were going to do. Mostly we avoided each other as much as possible the rest of the time in Vermont and on the ride home, let Samantha sit between us again. There was a bit of singing in the car, but none of it was by me or Kevin. When we said good-bye at their house, Kevin and I made eye contact for the first time in a while. He stared deep into my eyes and it is possible he was thinking that he loved me. Or that he was confused. Or that he hoped we could just forget what had happened, or that he was about to go call Tess and break up with her because he loved me so passionately. It was impossible to tell. Samantha hugged me good-bye. So did Joe. Kevin just stared. I got into the front passenger seat and rested my forehead against the cold window as we drove away.

I missed the first two days back to school, but managed to talk to Tess a few times on the phone without vomiting, which I considered progress. Apparently Kevin didn't break up with her or tell her anything that had happened between us because Tess was not only still talking to me but telling me how Kevin and she had been flirting so much by IM since we got back, and begging me to tell her if he had bought her a present while we were away. Luckily I was still feeling sort of weak, the postsick limpness that makes me more patient and less likely to interrupt, so I could let Tess go on and on about what she should do about Kevin, as well as her opinions regarding my mother, the wedding, what we should wear to it, and what life would be like afterward for us all.

The morning I got back to school, everybody was calling Kevin my brother. They seemed to think that was just the greatest thing. I nodded a lot. Which house were we going to live in (mine, since his actually is a rental, as Tess had said) and would his pool table go in my basement (still undecided at that point). It was exhausting. Even Mr. Hair-Man congratulated me. I couldn't look at him, in case he remembered the last time he said my name and Kevin's in the same sentence.

At lunch Tess continued to chatter about the wedding and the romance and how exciting it was. Darlene thought so too, though she also wanted to change the subject to the party she was having at her house a week from Saturday. I was pretty enthusiastic about discussing the party—anything to get off the subject of my screwed-up life. I listened happily to her rambles about what the theme should be, who should be included in the all-important setup, which people she hoped or dreaded would come, whether she should ask out Brad before the party or at it. I glanced at Jennifer when Darlene said that, but Jen turned away.

We headed out to the courtyard after Kevin swung by our table. Tess was holding hands with Kevin, walking between him and me toward the door. It was exactly what I had been picturing, dreading—and it felt even worse than I'd expected.

"You are both so moody," Tess said. "You should just get over yourselves and enjoy it, all the excitement and romance and possibilities for fun this brings up."

Yeah, well.

I didn't know where I stood with Kevin at all, although obviously we would not be going to the prom together, ever. I didn't know how I felt about him any more than I knew how he felt about me. Or even how I wanted either of us to feel. But I knew what had happened.

It didn't just happen either. I had wanted to kiss him; I had wanted him to kiss me. I'd wished for it; I'd willed it. I'd known he was going out with her at the time and what position that put me in. And I knew—I'd always known—what kind of person that made me.

He hadn't looked at me at all since we got back. I guess I'd known that was probably what would happen. I had tried to prepare myself for it.

My insides felt like shattered glass.

Tess turned to me, her hand still in Kevin's, and asked if I was happy.

"Happy?"

"A little happy? She's in love, your mom—don't you at least think that's romantic?"

"Oh," I said. "Sure."

"Are you?" she asked Kevin.

"Overjoyed," he said. "I'm gonna shoot some hoops."

Tess and I watched Jennifer and the boys play. I was thinking, too bad I'm not the girl my father had wanted, out there shooting hoops, everything clear—win or lose, the goal obvious, knowing which side you're on. Kevin went up for a layup and missed.

"He's so cute, isn't he?"

I shrugged. Every trail of conversation with my best friend hid land mines.

"I'm so whipped," Tess whispered. "I couldn't stop thinking about Kevin the whole vacation. It is such . . . it's so different from eighth grade."

"Do you feel like he fathoms you, though?"

"What? Does what to me?"

"Nothing. Something my mom said."

"Oh. She has some weird theories."

"I guess."

"But you have to tell me something, Charlie."

"What?"

"And I want you to remember that you were my best friend a long time before you got to be his almost-stepsister."

"Yeah," I said. "I remember."

"Tell me the truth. Did Kevin kiss anybody over vacation?"

"What?" I had to stretch my legs. I stood up. "Why, why, why do you think that?"

"He did, didn't he?" Tess stood up, too. "I had a feeling. Oh, man."

Here it was, then—and she was giving me a chance to come clean, to admit it, to apologize, to take whatever she dished out. "Tess," I said. My hands were shaking again, and I squeezed my fists tight. *This is a trauma of my own making,* I reminded myself. Why would anybody ever want to have a friend, when a friend might turn out to be like me? "The thing is . . ." How to begin? I'm sorry? I don't know how it happened, it just happened? More lies?

"Who did he kiss?"

That stopped me. She didn't know it was me?

"Tell me the truth—he kissed somebody on New Year's Eve, right?"

I couldn't believe it. I was getting off on a technicality. "No," I swore. "He did not kiss anybody on New Year's Eve. Except his little sister, maybe. I promise."

"Okay." She sniffled. "You promise? I had a whole story worked out. He met a girl in ski school, and she was beautiful . . ."

"I was the only one in his ski school class."

"Just you?" Tess looked relieved. She leaned lightly against me, the way Kevin had on the ski lift.

"Why . . ." I had to ask. I couldn't stop myself. "Why do you think he kissed somebody?"

"He's just acting kind of weird to me, since he got back. I don't know. Like awkward, or distant. So I starting thinking maybe he had fallen in love with somebody over the break."

"Really?"

"Yeah, or at least made out with somebody." She sighed. "I know you think he's a bit of a slut, Charlie, because of how many girls he's kissed. But he really means a lot to me."

"I know."

"Do you think he loves me, though?" she asked. "I told him I loved him."

"You did?"

"Yeah. We were online after you got back, and I told him, and he said, 'me, too.' Do you think that counts?"

All I could do was nod.

"Despite the fact that he's been acting weird? Or do you think it's that he's a little messed up, like you are, about your parents?"

"You think I'm messed up?"

"Deeply," she said, flinging her arm around me. "You are deeply messed up, my friend."

"You're right," I answered. "I am."

"Yup," she said. "So am I."

"You're not. You're perfect."

"We are all messed up," Tess said. "Each in our own unfathomable ways."

I slung my arm around her shoulder too, wondering if that was true. Was she as complicated as I was? Could she betray me the way I had betrayed her? The thought unsettled me completely, what we're capable of, any of us.

When the bell rang, Tess and I walked into school together, not chatting for once. We went to our lockers, to continue with our school day as if everything were normal, as if we still had confidence in ourselves and each other. Maybe she still had confidence. I realized there was no way for me to know for sure.

What I did know absolutely is that I was stuck. I hadn't told her. I knew now I could never tell her, not just because I am a wimp and weak and dishonest, but also because I had missed my chance. Telling her at some later point would mean admitting that, in addition to everything else, I hadn't been honest enough to come out with it right up front. In fact, I had pretty much denied it.

She could never forgive me for that. She *should* never forgive me for that. If I were her I'd never forgive me. She loves him. If she ever learned the truth, it would destroy our friendship.

So I could never tell her the truth.

But I also knew, because of the way I felt every moment

I spent with her since I got back from Vermont, that if I didn't tell her it would destroy our friendship anyway.

Maybe it was already destroyed and we just didn't know it yet.

# thirty-four

I SAT IN the cold Board of Ed room, waiting. Mom had to drop me off early because she had a meeting at six with a grad student about his dissertation. Mr. Lazarus offered to bring me after he picked up Kevin from basketball but I said no thanks, I'd rather go early. It was hard enough being around Kevin when I couldn't avoid it.

I didn't ask Tess to come. I was spending a little less time with her. I was spending less time with everyone, really. I was just doing my work and trying to think and say as little as possible. In the girls' room between classes, I overheard Tess explaining to Darlene that sometimes I get like this and just needed to have some space.

They didn't realize I was in the next stall, so I stayed very still, wondering what mean things they might say about me.

I was afraid to breathe or even pull up my pants. Tess started singing: *Personal space, personal space.* She taught Darlene the song and told her how cute my half brother is. "Almost as cute as her stepbrother," Darlene added, and Tess laughed her wicked laugh. Then they left. Nothing mean at all; they didn't know I could hear, and all Tess had done was support me.

The better a friend she was to me, the worse I felt.

At about a quarter to seven, people started filing into the boardroom. The only one I really recognized was Mrs. Buckley, the superintendent's wife, who sat down right next to me and said, "Hello, Tess!"

I managed not to cry.

At seven on the dot, Mrs. Buckley's husband, the superintendent, banged his gavel and called the meeting to order. He made a motion to dispense with the reading of the minutes, which somebody seconded. I have very clear notes on all this, which is how I can remember. I had rested in the afternoon so I wouldn't commit a repeat performance of last month's snooze fest, which is lucky because I noticed Mrs. Buckley sliding her eyes over to sneak a look at what I was writing. Wouldn't surprise me if ol' Mrs. Buckley took a little help from a pal now and then when she was a sly student herself.

Some woman named Pellodi or Pelloti was giving a presentation on tax revenue and distribution when there was a commotion at the back of the room. I was relieved at first because my eyelids were feeling ominously heavy. But then I saw who it was, and got sort of a bad feeling in my stomach.

It was a bunch of kids from the high school, mostly stoners who hang out on the Bridge. One was the guy who had looked jeeringly at me and Kevin that night at the ice cream place. The only other person I recognized specifically was George.

"Hi," he said, with a big goofy smile, as he passed by me, following the crowd.

"Hi," I mumbled back.

"What is this?" Mrs. Buckley muttered.

"No idea," I whispered back.

She and I sank into our seats as the crowd shuffled in and found seats in the empty first two rows. The board members looked a little worried, and Mr. Buckley banged his gavel to quiet everyone down.

"Mrs. Pellosi," he said, "please continue."

So she did, and the gang down front sat there quietly, listening. They sat through all the various items on the Board of Ed agenda, which I have, honestly, very few notes on because I was totally distracted. What were they doing here? What was going to happen? I could see the people up on the dais darting their eyes to them, repeatedly. Finally it happened.

Mr. Buckley banged his gavel and said, "Well, then, if there's no new business, I will entertain a motion to adjourn this—"

The scruffy guy from the ice cream store stood up, hands

in the pockets of his absurdly loose jeans. "I have new business to raise," he said.

Mr. Buckley peered down at him. "What is your name, young man?"

"Uh, Tony," he said. His friends chuckled. I wrote down *Tony?*

"Well, uh–Tony," Mr. Buckley said. "If you would like to address the Board, please remove your hat first."

Tony touched the visor of his dingy black baseball cap. Everybody waited. He lowered his empty hand. "Uh, no."

"Well, then . . ." Mr. Buckley banged his gavel.

"I got something to say," said Tony, louder. "I protest the banning of the anarchy and Frisbee clubs at the high school."

"This meeting is adjourned." *Bang, bang.*

"No," said Tony. "You have to listen. I am a student . . ."

"I don't have to listen to students," Mr. Buckley said. *Bang* went his gavel. "Ladies and gentlemen, this meeting is adjourned."

The high school students started yelling at the board members, some of whom were simply ignoring them and putting on their coats, but one of whom yelled back that they should learn some respect.

I was trying to take everything down. Mrs. Buckley leaned against my arm and whispered, "You have to deal with those rude teenagers every day, you poor thing?"

Then she got up and I guess found Mr. Buckley at the back. I had my head down over my pad. I wanted to make sure my notes were complete. This was my first big scoop. This was real news. The head of the Board of Ed had said, and I had the quote, "I don't have to listen to students."

I wanted to present both sides, all sides, of the story. I noted what everybody was wearing, exactly what Tony said, and exactly what Mr. Buckley said. This was going to be controversial, for sure. I had to have everything right. I understood for the first time what Mr. McKinley meant, about the free press being the most important part of a free society.

And in that room, I was the press.

It was a lot of responsibility, and a lot of power.

When I looked up, the room was almost clear, though I am pretty sure I saw George at the back, peeking in. He was gone by the time I got there, though. I rushed out to wait for Mom in the cold, but I didn't care. I sat down on the curb to write my first draft. My heart was pounding from the rush of it.

It felt almost like those moments when I fell in love with Kevin, only possibly even more exciting.

When Mom finally showed up, I got into the back seat so I could keep writing. I worked on the story until after midnight, writing and rewriting it, then got up at six to type it on my computer and edit it, making sure every word was right and necessary. I printed it out three separate times, after minor changes in each, but still I was at the bus stop ten minutes early, pacing in circles, clutching the article safe in a plastic folder.

I have never worked as hard on anything in my life, never been as excited about an assignment. I was breaking news. My legs were shaking as the bus bounced through town. Kevin didn't get on at his stop. I didn't care. All I could think about was this article. What a relief to be obsessed with something real, something important! It was great, it was perfect, it was the best thing I had ever written. I couldn't wait to submit it.

# thirty-five

I RAN OFF the bus and straight to the newspaper office before school started, without even finding Penelope first. I didn't want her to take my story, make some superficial revisions, and coast to Harvard on it. It was mine. I was scooping her after all. Ha!

Mr. McKinley was sitting there eating a doughnut, sipping steaming black coffee from a stained cardboard cup, reading the *New York Times*. When I opened the door, he bellowed, "Charles, my cub reporter. What have you got?"

"A scoop," I said, feeling a little silly but not fully.

"Oh, yeah?" He extended his beefy hand. "Let's see."

I handed it to him and stood there awkwardly beside him while he read my carefully typed page. Not an error on it, I was confident. I chewed on my lip.

Finally he lowered the page and nodded. "Not bad," he said.

I felt myself flush.

"There's a ninety-nine-year-old woman, used to be a librarian here in Winston years ago. Maybe you could do a feature on her. Penelope will give you the information."

"Okay," I said. "But what do you think about this, the article? How is it?"

"It's, well, you're improving. Good. I'll have Penelope edit it down."

I swallowed. "Why? Which . . . which parts do you think are—down to what?"

"Time and place."

"But what about the . . . the quotes? What they said? What Mr. Buckley said to Tony?"

"Oh," Mr. McKinley said. "We can't run that."

"Why not?"

"Well, for one thing, you didn't get Tony's last name. You can't run it without that."

"I'll get it," I promised. I tried to take a deep breath. "I'll get it. Anything else?"

"We can't run it, Charlie," he said.

"At all?"

He shook his head.

I felt my hands tighten into fists. "Why not?"

"We can't run the risk of misquoting a member of the Board of Ed."

"It's not a misquote." I kept my voice quiet and firm, in tight control. "I have it in my notes. I took it down as it happened, exactly as it happened!"

"Charlie, Charlie," Mr. McKinley said, standing up, his hugeness dwarfing me. "Do you know where this newspaper gets its funding?"

"No," I said, and then remembered. "The Board of Ed."

He shrugged. "Interview the old librarian. Don't be late to homeroom."

The bell rang. I didn't care. "What about the most important thing in a free society?"

"School is not a free society."

I punched the table. "You've got to be kidding me! This is news. This is the truth! You have to publish it! You have to! Or . . ."

He took a bite of his doughnut. A few crumbs fell from his lips. "Or what?"

"Or I will have to quit the paper," I threatened. I felt tears come to my eyes, as if newspaper had been the center of my universe.

"Okay," he said. "You're late to homeroom."

"And I will tell people. I will tell everybody, the whole school, what happened, and that you were too scared to publish it."

He glanced up at the clock, then took a swig of the coffee.

"And I'll tell the whole staff of the newspaper. We'll all walk out."

The second bell rang. Mr. McKinley sat back down and started reading his newspaper again. I stormed out of there and let the door slam behind me.

I was so mad I almost crashed into Kevin on my way down the hall.

"Hi, Chuck," he said.

"Hi," I said. "You won't believe what just happened. I wrote this article, this thing that . . ." I realized simultaneously that I had left the article I had written in the newspaper room with McKinley, and that Kevin had called me Chuck again. And, in fact, had actually talked to me for the first time since Vermont. I stood there with my mouth hanging open in front of him, unsure of what to do.

"I missed the bus," he said.

"Oh," I said. "So—the thing is? I wrote this really good article, for the paper, about what happened at the Board of Ed meeting and McKinley won't . . ."

Kevin knelt down and unzipped his backpack. "Are we late?" He looked up at me out of the corner of his eye. I could tell he was remembering the last time we got busted for tardiness. He gave me that smirk of his. It knocked the wind out of me.

"Kevin . . ."

"Phew. Here it is," he said, grabbing a folder out of his

bag. He stood up and hurried away from me.

"You're the one who . . ." I yelled after him. He rounded a corner and was gone, but that didn't stop me from yelling, "Hey! I am taking a stand for honesty, here! Hello?"

The bell to end homeroom rang and the halls were instantly flooded with the chaos of kids. Tess found me right away.

"Where were you?" She grabbed my arm and started pulling me toward English.

"Newspaper. You won't believe what happened." In a rush I told her what had happened as we walked toward English together. She looped her arm through mine, which made me feel very supported, especially in contrast to how Kevin had responded.

"Ew, those scruffy drug addicts who hang out on the Bridge?" she asked, when I looped back to what had actually gone on at the Board of Ed meeting.

"Yeah," I said as we got into English. "But that's not the point. Can you believe McKinley won't print it?"

"Well, if the Board of Ed is his wallet, you have to be realistic."

Ms. Lendzion told us to find our seats and quiet down.

"Realistic?" I couldn't believe her. "How about what's right?"

"Oh, please, Miss Crusader for the Truth," Tess whispered, her head close to mine. "So join chorus instead.

Newspaper is boring anyway. You said so yourself."

"Girls!" Ms. Lendzion yelled. "Eyes front, mouths closed, please."

I shut up, but I couldn't pay attention at all in English class. When the bell rang I was still fuming. And my best friend's Miss Crusader comment had not helped at all.

# thirty-six

I TRACKED DOWN Penelope and told her what had happened. She didn't sigh, which I took as a good sign; she nodded and listened, let me tell the whole story. "I left my copy of it in the newspaper room," I said. "Maybe you could get it for me, but if he already destroyed the evidence, I have it on my computer. I was thinking we should all quit."

"Quit?"

"In protest," I explained. "The whole staff of the newspaper."

"I have to get into college," Penelope said.

"What about freedom of the press? What about morality?"

"I can't think about morality until March."

Lunch was already halfway over. I decided to track down

everybody else I could find. If a big enough group of us walked off the newspaper, McKinley would have to listen—even if it wasn't everybody. Union now!

By the end of the day I did not have a large coalition. I had, so far, counting myself, one person willing to quit.

"You okay?" Jennifer asked me at our lockers at the end of the day.

"No," I said. "Would you quit newspaper with me?"

"Sure," she said. "Unless I have to join it first."

I slammed my locker shut. "Yeah, well."

"Is this about Kevin?"

"No!" I said, and ran out to the bus. For once it was NOT about Kevin. Jennifer of all people—she's the one who is supposed to NOT think everything is about boys! I really needed a walk but I had no time for the woods. I had a new idea—I would write a speech, present my case to everybody in a way that made it absolutely indisputable that I was right. Luckily Kevin wasn't on the bus to distract me—not that he could've. Bleh for self-involved him.

After ten bad starts and half a bag of Oreos, I decided I needed a break. I called my father. He's a lawyer. A small-town lawyer, it's true, with a specialty in real estate, but I guess I wanted some help crafting an argument and also maybe to show him that just because I am a klutz, it doesn't make me a bum. I had something I believed in, for once. He listened to my whole case, then gave his judgment, "Sounds like you're on the right side, Charlotte."

"Really? Thanks, Dad."

"Though, is this a teacher you're going to have at some point? You might not want to burn bridges."

"Whatever," I said.

"Listen, I'm glad you called," he said before I could hang up on him. "I want to talk to you about your mother."

I should never call him. I really should know better. "What?"

"I want you to give her a break, okay?"

"Give her a . . . what are you talking about? You are the one who's always going on and on about NOT giving people a break. And anyway, about what? A break from what?"

"She's worried that you feel . . . your mother is moving on with her life, Charlotte, and it's about time she looked up from her books, right? So buck up. You're practically an adult now. There's no excuse for moping around the house."

"Okay, Dad," I said. "Thanks, sorry, you're right, good-bye."

I couldn't even work on my speech anymore after that, I was so deflated. When Mom came home I was sprawled on the couch finishing off the last of our ice cream and watching the Lifetime channel.

"What happened?" she asked.

I told her. As she listened, she agreed and got angry, and I revived. "So what are we gonna do about this?" she asked.

"Maybe I could, I don't know, rally people?"

"Absolutely," she said.

She made dinner while I wrote my speech. I practiced it on her and she loved it. I designed a flyer while she ate (I couldn't eat, being both excited and also full of junk), and then we left the dishes in the sink and went straight to her office, where she made a hundred copies of my flyer that said "Censorship in our own Newspaper! Come to a Meeting at the Bridge, at lunch today, to hear the TRUTH!" She even stopped at 7-Eleven to buy me a fresh roll of tape so I could put them up all over school, and also some Twizzlers for the two of us to share. When we got home, she helped me put together the karaoke machine my grandmother in California sent me for Christmas last year, so I could bring it in and use the microphone.

"Mom?" I said, as I collapsed into bed.

"What?"

"Thanks."

"You're welcome."

"I'm happy for you, Mom. Joe is great. I really do like him."

"I knew you would. He likes you a lot, too, Charlie."

"And you."

She smiled. "And me." She kissed me on my forehead. "It'll all work out, baby. You'll see."

I closed my eyes, wondering if she meant my rally or our future, or both.

# thirty-seven

THE NEXT MORNING, Mom drove me to school. It took all my engineering ability, such as it is, to work the karaoke machine into my locker. I was in a sweat before I even started taping up the flyers. Through all my morning classes, I had to wrap my feet around the chair legs to keep me in my seat. When the bell rang for lunch I was already up. I scarfed down my sandwich in about two seconds. "Are you coming?" I asked my friends.

They kind of looked at each other but not at me.

"You sure you want to go to the Bridge, Charlie?" Tess asked. "Those people are so skeevy."

"I know," I said. "But don't you think this could be, like, a way to bring everybody together? Build a bridge, so to speak? They're involved. They're the ones who were silenced, and if we allow them to be silenced we'll all be silenced."

"A little silence would not be all bad," said Jennifer, who was bent over her bio textbook. "I'm gonna fail this test if I don't study."

"I quit smoking again," Darlene said. "But all I have to do is look at the Bridge and I'll start again. I'm going to the library." Her freshly scrubbed face looked apologetic. She really was making an effort, though school was not her best subject. She looked about eleven without her gold eye shadow.

"I'll go with you," Jennifer said to Darlene instead of to me. "Good luck, Charlie." They gathered their books.

"I should study too," said Tess.

"You never study at lunch!" I yelled after her.

"Try the decaf!" she yelled back. Darlene snickered.

*Fine,* I thought. *I'm independent, Mr. Lazarus said. George even once called me an independent thinker. So be it.*

I lugged the karaoke machine out of the cafeteria, down the hall, and out the door. Luckily it was a clear day, though cold and windy. I set the machine down, zipped up my jacket, and pulled on my hat and fuzzy red gloves. The Bridge was out there ahead of me, the most distinctive feature of the school. I had never gone anywhere near it. It was not my scene, completely off-limits to good girls like me.

I hauled the heavy machine down the walk and out onto the Bridge, set it down, plugged in the microphone, and turned it on. "Testing, testing," I said. Nobody looked up but I could hear for myself that it was on. "Testing, testing," I said again, really to get people's attention. A couple of stoners, a few feet away from me, looked up from whatever they were doing.

I dug into my backpack and pulled out the two pages of paper with my speech typed on them, double-spaced, fourteen-point Ariel font for easier reading.

"Hello. My name is Charlie Collins," I read, and then the wind ripped the papers out of my hands. They flew over the heads of all the people hanging out on the Bridge. We all watched the two papers sail away, doing a light, graceful dance with each other in the air.

I told myself I probably had it memorized anyway by now and started again. "Anyway. My name is Charlie Collins. I mean, hello, my name is Charlie Collins, and I am here today to let you know about a really bad problem, and the really bad . . ." I was a little lost. I hadn't written *really bad* twice.

I started over. "My name is Charlie Collins and I am here today to, to, today, to tell you, to alert you to the grave injustice of, the Board of Ed, a student tried to present, had, oh, and also our own school newspaper, because, well, a grievance, and the Board of Ed, a grievance was presented, I meant, to the Board of Ed—and the head of it, the Board of Ed, said, 'I don't have to listen to students!'"

I was panting. It was hard to figure out how to speak and

breathe at the same time. A couple of the guys, who, it has to be admitted, were in all truth very skeevy, as Tess had said, were watching me with some level of interest.

"Can you believe that?" I continued. "And when I, as a City News reporter, for our own, I'm the, um, on newspaper, they wouldn't, Mr. McKinley, who is all 'most important element' all the time, he . . ."

One of the stoners was standing right in front of me. "What?" I asked him, still using the microphone. "Was I talking too fast? Do you have a suggestion? My speech flew away; that was my speech, see those little white flying-up-there papers? So, should I start over, you think?"

He reached out and put his fingers on top of the microphone and gently pushed it down. He was the guy who had stared at me and Kevin back in the fall, at Mad Alice's. I recognized him. Uh—Tony. He was tall and lanky and, though he could have used a haircut, sort of handsome, up close.

"What?" I asked him again, unamplified.

"Could you stop yelling? It's really annoying."

"Don't you care that the Board of Ed won't listen to you?"

"Does anybody listen to you?"

"Well . . ."

"Nobody listens to me." He shrugged. "You get used to it."

"Sorry." I flipped off the karaoke machine and started to drag it back into school. It weighed a ton. The thought of maneuvering it back into my locker just overwhelmed me. I stopped, sat down on it, and felt tears well up. I was tired and alone, defeated and humiliated.

The bell rang to go back in to class, but I couldn't. I stood up and headed the other direction, to the woods.

# thirty-eight

RUNNING AWAY WHILE dragging a karaoke machine is quite a thing.

Running may be an overstatement. I had to stop every few steps to rest, but even so my arms were being pulled out of their sockets and stretched to gorilla length. I was even making gorilla noises. I thought I had sunk to my newest low point, when I heard someone's footsteps behind me.

I picked up the karaoke machine and made myself look straight ahead and not stop to rest, while lecturing myself on the unlikelihood of a bad guy lurking in Winston Woods, preying on girls who might cut school and walk home through the woods with ungainly luggage. I mean, even a bad guy would have to calculate the low odds of finding such a victim, right? Of course.

But the footsteps were gaining on me. I'm not fast at the best of times. *Don't look back, don't look back,* I told myself.

I could hear him getting closer. I had to make a decision. Keep the karaoke machine for use as a possible weapon of self defense, or lose it and run? I was never much of a singer anyway.

I dropped the handle and sprinted, jumping roots, dodging branches. One branch slashed across my face. I couldn't hear footsteps anymore, but I knew that could just be because I was breathing so loud. I was running for my life when I heard a loud voice say, "Charlie!"

How did he know my name? Was it on the karaoke machine? Was this a trick? A bad-guy lure to slow down gullible victims?

Again, "CHARLIE!" He was yelling my name into the karaoke microphone so loud he was getting feedback. Some predator—didn't even know how to use a microphone properly, I thought, and then it occurred to me that there was something familiar about the voice. I stopped and turned around.

"What are you doing?" said the voice. "You forgot your karaoke machine!"

I walked back toward him, and when I came around a big spruce tree, there he was: George.

"Hi," he said into the microphone. "I've always wanted to try one of these things." He jutted a hip out to one side and sang, "R-E-S-P-E-C-T! Find out what it means to me!"

"What are you doing here?"

"Following you," he said, as if that were obvious. "You didn't finish your speech."

I hung my head. "I didn't even start. You were there?"

"Yeah," he said.

"It was awful."

"Um, yeah. Pretty bad, as speeches go." He turned off the power and sat down on top of the machine.

I took off my backpack and sat down on it. "Mr. McKinley may as well have printed it. Nobody reads the City News section anyway."

"That's true." He wiped his nose. "Well, at least you're honest, and brave."

"I'm so not. I'm not brave and I am certainly not honest. That's what's wrong with you, George—you just see what you want to see."

"Really?" He considered that. "I thought it was my long torso."

"You thought *what* was your long torso?"

"The thing that's wrong with me." He stood up to show me, even unzipped his coat. He was right. He did have an unusually long torso.

"I hadn't noticed your torso before, particularly," I admitted. "It is long. Okay, that and your delusions."

"My delusions are—long?"

"Are what's wrong with you." I had to smile a little.

He rezipped his jacket and sat back down on my karaoke machine. "My delusions about what? You mean, how I think you're perfect but really you are lying and conniving?"

"Yes," I said. "That's right."

"When were you ever lying or conniving?"

"Trust me," I said.

"How can I trust someone who's lying and conniving?"

"George."

"By your own admission."

"Fine." I shook my head and formed the snow into a ball. "Believe what you want. You always have."

"Are you hating yourself because of that speech fiasco on the Bridge? Or because of Kevin Lazarus?"

I crushed the snowball. "What about him?"

"Yeah, I guess that is pretty bad. Okay. You're right. You're flawed. How shocking."

"What? What do you know?"

His mild smile faded away. "Everybody knows."

I took that in for a second. Whoa. "Everybody?"

"Yeah. I don't think I'm the one, by the way, who's deluded about your perfection."

The woods felt very quiet, and very cold. I wrapped my arms around myself. "Everybody knows what?"

"Well," he said, smiling mildly again. "Everybody except Tess, I guess."

"Oh, God. You do know. What do you know?"

He shrugged. "Do you have to buy special CDs for this thing, or does it use the regular ones?"

"George, please." I crawled over to him. "Everybody knows

what about me and Kevin? That I, that we, that I kissed him?"

"Well," George said. "For starters."

I put my head in my hands. This could not be happening. "You mean, that morning outside school, everybody knows about? Or what happened in Vermont?"

"Both." Oh, man. If everybody knew, it meant Kevin had to have told someone. Who? Only Brad, probably. Unless he was, like, bragging about it in the boys' locker room before gym—*hey, guys, you know what? I made out with Charlie while I was going out with Tess. Isn't that so cool?* No. Kevin may be slutty and selfish but he's not an idiot. But then, how could everybody know?

"How did you—George, please, you have to tell me. How did you hear about it?"

"You told me."

I was so confused. I looked up at him. "Me? When?"

"Just now."

"You tricked me?"

He shrugged. "Vermont, huh? That's gotta be awkward."

"So, wait. Nobody told you? You just, how did you know to say Kevin?"

"Your feelings for him were, ah, clear. It is so cold out here." He rubbed his hands together, then stood up and stamped his feet.

"It was that obvious?" I asked him, from down on the ground.

"Yeah," he said. He held out his mittened hand to help me up. I took it.

I dropped my head against his coat. "You think I should tell Tess?"

"Why would you?"

"If I don't, somebody else might."

"Maybe, maybe not. Let's think. Only you and Kevin know, right? And now of course you've told me. I could be paid to keep quiet, so there's just Kevin. And why would he tell her? So maybe she'll never find out. How much money do you have?"

"Why?"

"To keep me quiet. This is where we could meet for payments."

I shoved him. "Shut up. This is . . . George, I'm serious. This is, like, eating me up."

"The guilt? Because now, on top of it, you cut school. And forced me to cut too, which is a new one for me. I don't think I've ever been out here before. It's nice."

"If she finds out from somebody else, she'll never forgive me."

"She might not, anyway, even if you tell her."

"So what should I do?"

George shrugged. "Beats me. Why do you want to tell her so much?"

"Are you kidding?" I shoved him again. "Telling her is the last thing I want to do!"

"Really? Are you sure?"

"Are you crazy?"

"The possibility has crossed my mind."

We just stood there for a minute, facing each other in the cold woods. Puffs of breath from our mouths bumped into each other between us and merged. I looked up at George. He had on his knit cap, green-and-gray patterned, with a pompom on top and ear flaps. His cheeks were pink and his mouth had its usual half smile on it. I looked up into his dark brown eyes and for the first time I saw what my mother had meant. George was actually cute. Really cute. I found myself leaning slightly toward him.

*Oh man,* I thought. *I must be the most horny, hormonal creature on the entire planet.*

"Charlie," he said quietly. "Can I ask you something?"

"Uh-huh," I said, thinking, whatever else I do today, I cannot kiss George. I cannot get myself any more tangled up than I already am.

"Why did you do it?"

"Do what?"

"Kiss him."

"Kiss him? Kevin?" I took a step back, looked up at the trees. What a weird question, especially coming from George as I flirted with him.

"Yeah," he said. "Why?"

Was he mad at me, too? I guess he sort of had a right to be. But this was too weird. Why did I kiss Kevin? "Because, I don't know. Why are you asking me that?"

"I just wondered." He turned around and started walking.

"Where are you going?" I asked.

"Well, I don't know that many song lyrics, so I guess I'm done with karaoke for the day."

"George . . ."

He turned around. "Isn't there someone else you worry will never forgive you?"

"Who?"

He took off his backpack, set it in the snow, unzipped it, and pulled out a black book, a little bigger than an assignment pad. "This is for you." He tossed the book to me.

I clapped it between my gloved hands. "What is it?"

"A metaphor." He put on his backpack and walked away.

I looked down at the book in my hands. The cover was leather, smooth and black and blank. I opened it, and when I saw what was inside, I took off my gloves and dropped them on the ground. I sat down on the karaoke machine and looked slowly through the book. The weather report was glued down on each page, torn or cut from the upper right-hand corner of the newspaper, and, above it in George's scrawly handwriting, the date. Every day, one day after the other. December 16—Today, mainly sunny, less windy, high 46. Tonight, clouds thicken, low 41. Tomorrow, heavier rain arrives. December 17—Today, rain heavy at times, high 39. Tonight, partly cloudy, diminishing winds, low 29. Tomorrow, limited sun . . .

On and on, not a day missing, not even today.

# thirty-nine

THE THEME OF Darlene's party was: My parents aren't home.

She hadn't told any of us ahead of time for fear word would get out and people wouldn't be allowed to go, or her parents would somehow hear about it and cancel their weekend away. "You know the expression 'Three can keep a secret—if two are dead'?" she asked me, when I got dropped off.

I hadn't heard of it before. It didn't do a lot for my mood. I brought my sleeping bag and duffel up to her room. Tess and Jen and I were all planning to stay over. I wasn't sure how I felt about doing that with her parents not due back until the next day, but I didn't want to seem like a baby so I kept my mouth shut. I could always call my mom later if necessary. I went back down to help put chips in bowls.

It wasn't long after most people arrived that the bottle of gin from Darlene's parents' liquor cabinet started getting passed around. I had one sip from the Dixie cup Tess poured for me and almost puked on the spot. It tasted like liquid Band-Aids. Other people I guess did not agree.

"You just have to chug it," Tess told me. "Like this." She threw her head back and tossed the whole shot of liquor into her mouth at once. Swallowing, she made a terrible face, then smiled. Kevin smiled at her and shook his head, then kissed her lips lightly.

I threw my head back and tossed my drink in, too. It burned, it was bitter, it was disgusting. For a few seconds I was unsure if I'd be able to force myself to swallow it and, once I did that, whether I'd be able to keep it down. But I did. So there.

"See?" Tess said. "Isn't that better?"

I crumpled my cup before she could pour me any more.

"Let's bake," she said. "C'mon, Kevin, let's see what there is to bake." He followed her. She flipped her head back to look at me, her blond hair catching the light. "Aren't you coming, too, Charlie?" She gave me a little pout with her lip-glossed mouth. She still had some on, then. She hadn't done all that much kissing yet. I knew I was being mean, if only in my own head. I had been internally nasty toward her ever since she went to the library instead of coming with me to the Bridge. As if I had any right to question her loyalty to me. But there it was.

I followed them to the kitchen. Loud music was playing in every room, different songs all smashing together. It was hard to think through the noise and the buzziness that must have come from that horrible stuff she'd made me drink—what was it? Gin. Oh, yeah. Beaten again. *I should know I'm no good at gin by now,* I thought, which made me smile.

"What?" Kevin was looking at me.

"What what?" I asked him.

"You had a . . ." he whispered. Man, his whispering really kills me. "Nothing. Hey. Mr. McKinley asked me to tell you something."

I raised my eyebrows at him, unsure whether the heart palpitations had to do with him or with newspaper or both. "What?" I asked.

"He said he re-read your article and if you want to reconsider quitting the paper, he'd be willing to take you back."

"How grand of him," I said. "But he won't publish it, will he?"

"No." Kevin shrugged. "Who cares? It's just the school paper, Chuck."

"Chuck?" Tess asked. "That's cute. I like it. Chuck. Chuck, help me get up on the counter." She took another swig of gin, then grabbed my hands, made them into a step for herself, and climbed from my palms onto the counter.

I felt myself grimacing at her behind her back. I tried to shake myself out of it, reminding myself that she was my best friend, and even if this is one side of her I don't enjoy so much, this fun-loving-party-girl-flirtatious side, well, there are sides of me that are even worse so I should have some patience and tolerance. We all suck, especially me.

She threw down a box of brownie mix. "Score!" She jumped down and crashed lightly into Kevin, who caught her. "Whew," she said. "Guess I've had enough." She picked up her cup from the counter and handed it to Kevin. "You have it."

She crossed her arms and leaned back against the counter where I was already leaning with my arms crossed. Her and me, a team, as always. We watched Kevin look into the cup, swirl the clear liquid around a couple times, then chug it. "Ugh," he said, screwing up his face. "Bleh. That stuff is lighter fluid."

Tess laughed her wicked laugh and got busy making the brownies. I helped; a bunch of people helped. She has a way of deputizing everybody. She was just bugging me, I guess.

About fifteen minutes after the brownies started baking she opened the oven door to check on them. "I think they're ready," she announced, and took them out, her butt up in the air.

"They're not ready," I said. I grabbed the box out of the garbage to show her. "It's thirty-four to thirty-seven minutes, if that's a nine by nine pan. If it's eight by eight, it's forty-two to forty-five. They've been in for fifteen! They're still liquid."

"They're still liquid," she mocked. "Listen to you,

Chuckie. When did you become Chef Boyardee?" She was rummaging through drawers. She pulled out a spoon and shoved it into the hot brownie goo. She blew on it a few times, then put it in her mouth.

"That's disgusting," I said. "You ruined them."

"Come on, Betty Crocker," she said, tossing the spoon onto the counter beside the pan of half-cooked brownies. She looped her arm around my shoulders and leaned toward Kevin, dragging me with her. "Don't judge your stepsister-to-be when she gets like this, Kevin. Deep down inside, she is not as serious and self-righteous as she seems. It's just a phase. Charlie can actually be a lot of fun."

"He knows," I said. And I felt a wave of cold slide down me, from her arm on my shoulder down to my toes. Cold, cold, cold.

"What?" Tess asked, cocking her head at me.

"He knows I can be fun. Ask him."

"You know she can be fun? Kevin?"

Kevin looked a little pale. The room had gotten quiet, I think. Everybody seemed to be leaning forward, listening.

"Sure," he said, shrugging.

Tess leaned toward Kevin and kissed him on the mouth, a teasing little kiss, light but lingering. Her arm was still around me so I was dragged in near the kiss myself. "Mmm. You just need to get kissed, Charlie. You are so tense lately."

"Shut up, Tess," I said.

"What? It's true."

"It doesn't matter." I said.

"Really?" Tess smiled at everybody in the kitchen. "It doesn't matter? Says the Crusader for the Truth? The Kamikaze Karaoke Truth Crusader?"

She laughed her wicked laugh. I didn't laugh with her, didn't crack a smile. I couldn't look around, knowing all our friends were watching this. Knowing George was behind us by the fridge, and Jennifer over by the pantry. *Please stop*, I begged Tess silently; *hold it in*, I begged myself.

"Come on, Charlie, I'm just kidding. Can't you take a joke? I'm sorry." She tried to kiss me on my cheek. I pulled away. She picked up Kevin's hand and held it. "She won't even kiss me. She's never going to kiss anybody. She is purity itself." She leaned in to kiss him again.

"That's not true," I said.

Tess pulled her mouth away from Kevin's, or maybe he pulled away from her. I couldn't really tell.

"Really?" Tess asked. "Who are you going to kiss?"

"Kevin."

Her face went white and, though she was trying to smile, the effort showed more than her teeth.

"Actually, I already kissed him."

Well, that stopped everything. Too late now. Her eyes were open wide, and I was on a roll.

"Yeah, there it is. I kissed him. You wanted to know who he kissed over vacation? Me. He kissed me, not on New Year's Eve, that's my technicality—but he kissed me. Deep and wet. I kissed him and it was great. You wanted to know who he fell in love with over vacation? It was me. So you can stop flicking your pretty hair around and encouraging me and Kevin to get along, because we do get along, sometimes too well."

Tess blinked twice, then looked at Kevin, who was looking at his feet. She let go of his hand and walked out of the kitchen then up the stairs. We all watched her go.

Darlene put on the pot holders and picked up the brownies. "These really do need more time," she said, and slipped them back into the oven. That seemed to unglue everybody, because they all dashed out of the kitchen, whispering to one another as they headed for places to sit down and rehash the scene I'd just caused. Kevin went into the bathroom and locked the door. I decided I needed a little personal space so I whipped past George, who was still leaning against the fridge watching me.

I grabbed my coat from the closet, went out the front door, and sat on the step to breathe some cold air. The book from George was in my pocket. I ran my fingers over the smooth cover and tried not to think.

A few minutes later, the door opened. Tess came out. She had her duffel and sleeping bag. Her eyes were red.

"Where are you going?" I asked, my voice croaky.

"My mom's coming," she said. "I called her."

I nodded. "Tess . . ."

"Shut up."

"I'm sorry."

"I don't care," she snapped.

A thousand explanations, justifications, arguments popped into my head. I kissed him first, I tried to tell you, it just happened, it didn't mean anything, you hurt me sometimes, too, it will never happen again. Even the few that were true didn't excuse me, though. I had nothing to offer. I just sat there silently, torturing myself with the knowledge that this was probably the last moment we'd ever spend alone together.

"Why?" she asked, after a few minutes.

"I don't know," I said. "George asked me the same thing."

"You told George? How many people do you want to stab? What is wrong with you?"

"I'm crazy. Stupid. Selfish. I don't know."

"And . . . why?"

"Lust? Love? Desire?" I tried to think, to be honest. "I guess, I wondered about it. I wanted to feel it, to experience how it would feel if we, you know, kissed—and, for the first time I was feeling the awesomeness, the overpowering—that's how you said it felt—overpowering. Indescribable. I didn't know what to do with the—I was overpowered, maybe, by the feelings."

She sniffed. "You love him that much?"

"No," I said. "I don't think so."

"But you hate me that much."

"No," I said. "The only one I hate is myself. I love you."

"No you don't. Not if you could do this to me. Not if you could betray me, all these times, not just when you kissed him, not just tonight, but every conversation, you just kept betraying me, your best friend. I'm the best friend you've ever had."

"Yes," I said. "You are."

"I *was*."

I started to cry. I tried to stop, to hold it in. She had every right to say that, I reminded myself. I knew the price; I'd always known.

"What did I ever do to you?" she asked. "I really want to know. What?"

"Nothing." I took a breath, and answered the only truth that occurred to me. "You just . . . were . . . one notch better."

She shook her head. "I have no idea what you're talking about."

"Yes you do," I said, and cleared my throat. "We both know, we've both always known. You are the prettier one, the more confident, the more fun, the more talented one. I'm *almost* as much, always *almost*. It's not your fault, I'm not blaming you. I'm just saying, if we're being completely honest here, that's always been the thing, you—and then me. And that was always fine with me, I didn't mind, or I didn't think I did—but maybe a little bit, I did."

"So you kissed Kevin just to get back at me."

"No, not just," I said. "There's also a thing between me and Kevin. I'm sorry, but there is, which is obviously, and not just because of you, going to have to be eliminated. Maybe it already is. I don't think I love him, really. Kevin is more . . ."

"Forget Kevin," Tess said. "What is that, like, a boy fantasy, to make out with best friends? Please. But he's just a boy. You were my best friend."

I nodded. Were.

"And you what, wanted to bring me down a peg?"

"No. Not that. I just, I wanted to be chosen. Instead of you."

"Well, congratulations," she said, looking away from me. "You win."

The tears ran down my face. I didn't care; I didn't wipe them away. "Will you ever forgive me?"

Her mom's car pulled into the driveway. Tess picked up her stuff. "I don't think so," Tess whispered as she passed me.

# forty

THE LAKE HAD thawed and buds dotted all the trees around it. Samantha's hair was done in long ringlets with baby's breath threaded through, and mine was pulled back on top in complicated twists, but blown out straight and shiny beneath. I agreed to lip gloss and mascara. Sam got only gloss. Kevin and his dad were wearing identical suits, except for the sizes. And my mother looked more beautiful than ever. Her dress was plain, a pale pink sheath, and she wore a wreath of flowers in her hair, but it was her face that was remarkable. She couldn't stop smiling. I asked her if her cheeks felt sore as we checked ourselves in the mirror before heading downstairs. "Very," she said.

Samantha came out of her room, which used to be the old TV room. She had declared she was absolutely not getting rid of the wallpaper in there because she absolutely loved the little jungle animals on it. I had picked that wallpaper. I smiled at her and told her she looked great. She arranged her legs into an awkward stance like my own and shrugged. "Whatever," she said, but her random-toothed smile gave away her cool.

I squeezed her around the shoulders and we headed downstairs, past the closed door of Kevin's room. He and Joe were downstairs shooting pool in the basement, killing time. Our basement, now—all of ours.

The social whirl had calmed down somewhat after Darlene's party—not because of my outburst, either. That was overshadowed for most people by the fact that a bunch of kids drank so much they threw up all over Darlene's living room just as her parents came home early and surprised everybody who was still there. Pretty much the whole grade was grounded for a while, and things hadn't picked up all the way, since. Jennifer and Brad had started chatting more, and he even beat her twice at basketball, but so far, as far as anyone knew at least, no kissing. Though I suppose you never know.

A couple of times George walked me home, through the woods. Sometimes we talked, but sometimes we just cracked sticks or tossed rocks into the stream. It was nice.

I missed Tess so much it ached.

I sent her an invitation to the wedding, of course. She didn't RSVP. Friday in the hall, she nodded at me, I think, or else her head had just bobbed coincidentally. But for once she didn't turn away. That's something. That had to mean something, I told myself.

Joe walked down the aisle first, between Kevin and Samantha. They all looked beautiful. Kevin and Samantha stood up on the platform and turned to face us. Joe waited on the ground and smiled his slow smile as my mother and I started down the aisle. We stopped halfway there, as we'd practiced, and I gave her an air kiss near her cheek. "Charlie," she whispered.

"What?" If she was panicking I'd run with her back up the aisle and we could ditch our shoes and hike down the hill, home.

"You're my number-one love, and you always will be."

Tears sprouted in my eyes. I tried to suck them in but eyes are not all that well suited to sucking. "Mine, too," I croaked. "You, I mean." And I continued down the aisle to stand under the canopy across from Samantha and Kevin, passing Joe, who was on his way up the aisle to join my mother.

The party afterward was fun. The Association made an exception and let us use the clubhouse, which was decorated in a wedding theme. There was a DJ playing decent music, mostly old stuff, but okay. I danced with Joe, and with George, who had come as my sort-of date. While I danced with George, Kevin danced with Samantha. Tess had dumped him, of course, and he hadn't asked anybody else out since. I guess we all needed a break from love.

The next dance, Joe asked Samantha. I figured that was Kevin's cue to ask my mother, but he turned to me instead and held up his arms. What could I do? I stepped into Kevin's personal space and felt his arms close loosely around me.

We didn't talk, didn't make eye contact. That was our way now, even when we weren't dancing together with a roomful of adults watching us. It felt weird and distant yet familiar, like what had happened between us was a long time past. I was thankful for that. The slight heart-thudding was like an aftershock from an earthquake, I figured, and aftershocks are natural, expected, and always diminish in power with time.

The song ended and I left quickly to get a drink from the bar. An orange juice. I had made a vow never to drink alcohol again—especially gin, ever. The sun was setting so I walked out onto the deck to look at it, over the lake. Nothing like lake-looking to dilate the mind.

"Charlie."

It was Tess, down below the deck. She was in shorts and a T-shirt, her bike between her legs, her helmet unbuckled on her head.

"Tess."

"Congratulations."

"Do you want to come in? Get a drink? Did you get the invitation? You were invited, Tess. I swear I . . ."

Tess nodded, then shook her head. "Tell your mom I send my love."

"Okay."

"You okay?"

"Yeah," I said. "You?"

"Yeah."

"So, um . . ."

"So." She buckled her helmet. "I just wanted . . ." She shrugged.

"Thanks. You're the best."

"No I'm not," she said. "I'm just . . ."

"Okay."

"Okay."

She jumped up onto the pedals of her bike and sped away. I watched her go until I couldn't see her anymore. Inside, people were clapping. I looked up at the endless, cloudless sky.

Someone tapped my shoulder and I turned around. George. He'd surprised me again. I felt myself smile at him, and watched him return it.

"Want to walk a bit?"

I nodded, set down my glass on the railing, and led him toward the woods. We walked awhile. I was thinking I should ask him if he was having a good time, thank him for coming, something polite. Instead I asked, "Is it you?"

"Who?" he asked, and pointed at his chest. "This? No, this is someone else entirely."

I shook my head. "It's you I should also be asking to forgive me, right?"

"Why me?"

"Because," I stammered. "Because you, at the time, when I, when Kevin and I . . ."

"Oh, that again?" George shrugged. "No. It had nothing to do with me."

"So you weren't mad, then?"

"At you? Why would I be?"

"You know," I said. Why did he always have to torture me? "Because Kevin and I . . ."

"Kissed?"

"Yeah."

"No."

"It didn't bother you?"

"No."

"Because . . ." Oh, how embarrassing to figure it out at this late stage, especially with him there as my date. "Because you didn't, I mean don't, like me in that way." I smiled to show no big deal, I always knew that, I haven't been flattering myself into thinking otherwise all this time.

"Oh, no," George said. "I liked you in that way. In the kissing way? Oh, I liked you, I like you, very much, in that way exactly. I always have."

I was so confused. "So then . . ."

"All right, it bothered me a little. But I knew I had to be patient, and . . ." He touched my shoulder. "It's you. You have to ask to forgive—yourself."

"Me?"

"It's always been you," he said. His face was all a question. I put my hands behind his back, pressed against his jacket with my palms, tilted my face up to his, and kissed him.

It wasn't at all like kissing my cousin, or Kevin. It was soft and sweet and romantic and even under a tree. And in the background, up the hill at my mother's wedding, music was playing. George touched the side of my face with his palm and pulled back, his eyes still closed. He opened them slowly and said, "I didn't care who kissed you first as long as I kissed you last."

We eventually made it back to the party, holding hands. Everybody was still having a good time. It was a good party, and I had come to seriously hate parties. At one point the guests picked each of the five of us up in chairs and gave us rides around the room, which was more harrowing than fun. After that, Mom and Joe cut the cake, and then the good-byes began. Mom and Joe were postponing their honeymoon until the summer, when we kids would be away at camp, so the five of us were the last to leave.

Joe carried Samantha half-asleep up to bed, and I helped Mom untangle the wreath from her hair. "You looked beautiful tonight, Mom," I told her reflection in the mirror. "Heck of a night."

"Thank you, Charlie," she said. "Thank you for being my best woman. You are, you know. You're the best woman I know."

I didn't want to ruin her night by explaining to her why I am so not, why I am so far from the best woman, or even a good woman, or even a woman. Well, but I am not a little girl anymore either, I guess. I said, "Thank you, I love you, good night," the mother-daughter greatest hits.

I hung up my dress on the special hanger it came with and pulled on my flannel nightgown. I was tired. I was tired from the whole year. I headed for the bathroom to wash up. My hair got a little wet as I started to wash my face. I wanted to try to keep the twists in for the after-wedding brunch in the morning, not mess myself up so fast. What to do?

I pulled off my underwear and put it on my head. Just as goofy-looking as Tess, I saw in the mirror, and almost as pretty. No. Not almost. Different. Goofy and pretty and obviously still deeply messed up. I finished washing up and put my underwear back where it belonged. It was clearly time for bed.

When I opened the bathroom door, Kevin was in his doorway, staring at me.

I was startled. I stared back. We stood those few feet apart, in our pajamas, frozen. He was probably just waiting to go brush his teeth, I realized, and turned away, went back down the hall to my room. The thumping of my heart would just take a minute to subside, I knew, so I sat on my bed with my eyes closed and waited. I congratulated myself on getting used to this chemical stuff.

When the thumping calmed, I opened my eyes. There was Kevin, standing inside my doorway. His chest was expanding, contracting under his white T-shirt as he moved two steps closer to me.

I stood up. "Kevin . . ."

"Chuck," he said. "I . . . you . . . I wanted to . . ."

"What?"

He lifted his right hand, touched his pointer lightly to my forehead, and whispered, "North."

A Global Kiss. He was giving me a Global Kiss. My mind sped forward. I knew what was coming, I knew the end of the Global Kiss: *I love you all over the map. I love you. . . .* I felt my legs starting to shake. Do I love him?

He touched my chin. "South."

What should I do? It would be so bad, so deliciously bad, if . . .

My cheek. "East." If we do this, if we kiss . . .

Other cheek. "West." Do I love him all over the map? No. I smiled. It was simple and clear, and George's face was in my mind. But even that wasn't what pulled me back to the shore of sanity. I had stopped spinning.

He opened his eyes, his dark blue eyes, deep as the lake, and stared into mine. We waited, both of us, wanting and waiting to see what would happen. I leaned forward, a little, toward him. He leaned forward too. I do like these feelings, these powerful new charged feelings, but they don't belong to him.

We met in the middle. One of us, I'm not sure which, made a humming sound, or maybe it was a sigh. I think it was me.

I kissed him, lightly, on the forehead, and pulled away.

# if we kiss

# A Q&A with Rachel Vail

**Q:** Why did you decide to write a story about a first kiss?

**A:** Is this a story about a first kiss? I guess it is. Hmm. The thing is, that's not how I write. What I do is, I make up characters and figure out who they are and what they want, need, are afraid of, or regret— and then imagine what could happen to them that tests all they believe about themselves. So this is a story about a girl named Charlie, who has never kissed anybody, who has convinced herself she has no interest in being swept away by the passionate feelings of falling in love for the first time.

**Q:** Do any elements of *If We Kiss* come from real-life experiences?

**A:** Absolutely. Some of the details come from my own life, or from lives of friends or things I overhear on the subway or in grocery stores, or from letters or e-mails kids write to me. Some plot points are imagined or cobbled together from many sources. But every feeling that any character experiences is a feeling I have felt myself. For example, though I never fell in love with a guy who then became my stepbrother (and in fact don't have a stepbrother) I have certainly felt my heart pound for a completely inappropriate guy, and been simultaneously ashamed and intrigued by the feeling.

**Q:** What was *your* first kiss like?

**A:** I was in the play *Bye Bye Birdie* and my real-life boyfriend was playing the part of my boyfriend in

3

the show. We had held hands a couple of times and I remember to this day how his hand felt—big, soft, and warm. Opening night of the play, when we were in the wings on opposite sides of the stage about to come out for our bows, I saw that he had flowers for me. We met center stage and as I tried to grab the bouquet, he leaned forward and planted a big soft kiss right on my lips. Ack! I was so surprised, I did what I usually did when a relative landed a kiss on my mouth—I wiped it off with the back of my hand. My father filmed the whole thing. My first kiss: wiped away in front of hundreds of people and preserved forever on family film.

**Q:** So your first kiss was pretty much the opposite of Charlie's. She keeps hers a secret for most of the book—do you think secrets like that are bad or good?

**A:** Both.

**Q:** How did you and your husband first meet? Was he a "Kevin" (i.e. someone you shouldn't date) or a "George" (someone who had always been right in front of your nose), or something else entirely?

**A:** We met in elementary school. We were friends for many years before we even thought about each other romantically, and then it was about ten more years before we started dating. Thank goodness. He is sort of a combination of George and Kevin—sweet and smart but also irresistible and charismatic.

**Q:** Did you ever regret kissing someone?

**A:** Oh, yes.

**Q:** Have you ever had to betray your best friend, possibly for a guy? Do you consider that kind of betrayal wrong, or just part of growing up, or what?

**A:** It is wrong to betray a friend, and it is even worse to betray yourself or your ideas of who you would like to be. You never *have to* do that. Part of growing up is recognizing that feeling attracted to somebody, or discovering that somebody is attracted to you, does not mean you MUST act on it. It can be a lovely feeling that you (powerfully) walk away from.

**Q:** Have you ever had a really good friend, like Tess, that you wanted to be more like? What were you envious of, and how did you deal with it?

**A:** Often. I try to surround myself with people I admire; I consider myself incredibly lucky to be surrounded by people I want to be more like. I try to listen to them, watch them, see what it is that they do well—and then either learn from them or just appreciate their gifts (marathoning, painting, and singing in operas—things I will never do, for instance). When I catch myself feeling envious, I try to remember to count my blessings, and then I feel like oh, great, I'm also petty and envious and shallow . . . so I have a little hate-myself party for a few minutes until I am bored and over it.

**Q:** What's your favorite thing about kissing?

**A:** I could never choose just one thing.

# Rachel on How *If We Kiss* Began

**C**HARLIE'S STORY STARTED with her voice. She sounded, in my mind, blunt and honest, devoid of apology or excuses. Originally her name was Mallory. She had a twin sister named Meredith and a best friend named Anne, a boyfriend named George and a huge disastrous crush on, you guessed it, Kevin. I wrote a short story called "One Hot Second" that appeared in the collection *Thirteen*. And that, I thought, was that. But Mallory stayed alive in my mind, and grew, and changed, and, in her calm but unrelenting way, demanded to be written about more. Names were changed, events reorganized, characters (Anne and Meredith, for example) merged and morphed and reimagined . . . until the story became *If We Kiss*. But here, so you can see how it changed and how it didn't, is the beginning of "One Hot Second."

## <u>one hot second</u>

ABOUT A MONTH OR SO ago I dumped this kid named George. He cried in the cafeteria. It was horrible. I almost said I'd go back out with him right then and there, just to get him to stop. I can't handle scenes. But I didn't like George anymore. I liked a kid named Kevin. A week after I dumped George, Kevin asked me out and of course I said yes. There is one problem with Kevin. He's a little fast. He French-kissed his last girlfriend twelve times in one dance, but I tried not to let it bother me. I really wanted to kiss him and I knew he wanted to kiss me, but I didn't know he was horny enough to want to do it in the hall.

Well, a week after I started going out with Kevin, I found myself standing in the hall, between fifth and sixth block, with my arms around him and my tongue in his mouth. It was really disgusting but I liked it.

It was my first kiss.

I'd had this idea about waiting and George respected that. He may have thought it was weird but he never acted that way. He just said he respected that I was an independent thinker and pure person and he would wait until I was ready. George is a real gentleman. Mothers like George. Good old George.

Anyway I got sick of waiting. I couldn't remember what exactly it was I was waiting for. I wanted to kiss somebody and fall in love. My twin sister Meredith has fallen in love with all three boys she's kissed, and she said there was no way I could possibly understand how awesome and overpowering that kind of love is without experiencing it for myself. She said it was beyond describing. I realized that in my entire life every single experience had been describable. In fact, I'd described most of them to Meredith.

I had some romantic ideas about how my first kiss would happen. Maybe a willow tree, maybe some music. Kissing George would've been like kissing my cousin. Totally describable. Plus, I didn't want to tell him. He'd think I was horny and not so interesting and different and pure as he'd imagined. I didn't want to disappoint George.

Kevin scrunches his eyes when he looks at you. He leans

close. The day before I dumped George, Kevin had stopped in front of me in the hall and asked me if I was ready for the bio quiz. While he was asking, he touched my hair. It was a strand on the front left side. He twirled it around his index finger and then let go. When he did that I couldn't remember if I was even taking bio this year. I think I may actually have said, "duh." Kevin smiled and strolled into class. I sat down on the floor and realized I had to dump George.

The only reason it took me until the next day to do the dumping was because for the rest of that afternoon I was too stupid to talk, and way weak in the legs.

Two weeks later I was pressed up against a locker kissing Kevin. The lock was digging into my backbone, but I didn't want to wreck my first kiss by readjusting. I squeezed my eyes shut and tried to concentrate.

**For more of "One Hot Second," look for it in the short story anthology called *Thirteen*, edited by James Howe.**

# Take a Kissing Quiz
### Ever wonder, what would happen if we kiss?
*Take this quiz to find out what your kissing style is, and then . . . get out there and try it!*

1. **Charlie describes French kissing as "disgusting and wonderful." How would you describe it?**
   (a) Intimate and profound.
   (b) Sexy and strange.
   (c) Uncomfortable and a waste of time.
   (d) Cool and sophisticated.
   (e) Yummy and fun.

2. **Practicing smooching on your pillow is**
   (a) Ridiculous.
   (b) Great—my pillow really loves me, at least.
   (c) Messy. Is that a clean pillowcase? Does drool stain synthetic fabrics?
   (d) Sadly, the closest you'll ever to the real thing.
   (e) Useful!

3. **After your first kiss with someone, your instinct is to**
   (a) Hold hands, of course.
   (b) Run away, blushing, and hope no one saw!
   (c) Assuming you liked it, move on to your second kiss!
   (d) Call your best friend ASAP, and give her all the details.
   (e) Savor the moment privately. Was it "indescribable," as Tess would say?

**4. Your biggest kissing fear is**
(a) That you suck at it.
(b) Germs, germs, germs.
(c) That you're a slut now.
(d) That he doesn't really love you.
(e) That it'll be boring, and the guy will get all clingy.

**5. Kevin does this humming/sighing thing while kissing. If a boy ever did that while kissing you,**
(a) You'd be slightly grossed out. Why all the sound effects?
(b) You'd hope it means he thinks you're the one.
(c) You'd probably groan a little too, to keep up.
(d) You'd be totally into it.
(e) You'd worry he regretted kissing you. Were you really that bad?

**6. You prefer being kissed**
(a) In a dark closet.
(b) When it's a total surprise.
(c) When you know it's coming: there's flattering lighting, you've brushed your teeth a few times, and you're wearing the right outfit.
(d) At a party where there are usually other people doing it.
(e) In the caf, the school parking lot, or anywhere else public—if you've got it, flaunt it!

**7. If you were in the same situation as Charlie and liked your best friend's boyfriend, would you kiss him over winter break, too?**

    (a) Yes, romance always comes before friendship.

    (b) Yes, you have to be true to your own feelings first.

    (c) No way, you'd never kiss your friend's boyfriend. That's no way to get a boyfriend, it's just the way to lose a friend.

    (d) No, you'd be too nervous about getting caught or people thinking you're a slut.

    (e) Maybe. But if you did, you'd feel really bad about it, too.

**8. You'd rather kiss**

    (a) An off-limits boy, like Kevin.

    (b) A boy you've known and trusted forever, like George.

    (c) An almost-complete stranger, like a guy on the newspaper staff, or one of those kids who hangs out by the bridge.

    (d) Whatever celebrity you're obsessed with at the time.

    (e) No one, really—you just don't see what's so great about the whole kissing thing.

**9. My very first kiss was . . .**

    (a) Surprising, slobbery, and icky.

    (b) You were so excited to be kissing you barely

noticed what happened.

(c) Pretty romantic.

(d) Awkward, but not so bad.

(e) Hasn't happened yet—still waiting!!!

## 10. It seems like people usually kiss because

(a) They're attracted to each other.

(b) They just love to kiss.

(c) To show off that they have someone to kiss.

(d) Their friends are doing it so they think they should, too.

(e) They want to feel closer to one another.

## 11. What produces the F.K.G. (Freshly Kissed Glow)?

(a) Happiness.

(b) Hormones.

(c) True love.

(d) Embarrassment.

(e) Fever, possibly mono.

## 12. The best kisser is probably someone

(a) H-o-t-t!

(b) Trustworthy.

(c) Intense.

(d) Experienced.

(e) Sensitive.

# SCORING:

1. (a)3 (b)4 (c)1 (d)2 (e)5 2. (a)2 (b)5 (c)1 (d)3 (e)4 3.
(a)2 (b)1 (c)5 (d)4 (e)3 4. (a)4 (b)2 (c)1 (d)3 (e)5 5. (a)2
(b)3 (c)4 (d)5 (e)1 6. (a)1 (b)4 (c)3 (d)2 (e)5 7. (a)5 (b)4
(c)2 (d)1 (e)3 8. (a)4 (b)3 (c)5 (d)2 (e)1 9. (a)2 (b)5 (c)3
(d)4 (e)1 10. (a)5 (b)1 (c)2 (d)4 (e)3 11. (a)5 (b)4 (c)3
(d)2 (e)1 12. (a)5 (b)3 (c)4 (d)2 (e)1

## (12–24) Cryptic Kisser

Let's be blunt: Kissing is, well, a little WEIRD! I mean,
someone's getting in your personal space and basically
wagging their tongue at you, only it's supposed to be all
meaningful. Don't worry, you WILL find someone who
you really want to kiss.

## (25–36) Charming Kisser

To you, kissing has the potential to make dreams come
true. But don't be scared to take a risk on someone
you never thought of that way before (like George!).
The best thing about kissing is it allows you to surprise
yourself.

## (37–48) Curious Kisser

Kissing can be romantic, kissing can be weird, kissing can be just plain fun. After a few kisses and a few
intense conversations with friends about it, you've pretty
much figured that out for yourself. But you want more.
Think about it, what are the things YOU love about
kissing?

## (49–60) Cuckoo for Kissing

Okay, so you're one of the girls in the hallway smooching their boyfriends against the lockers, aren't you? Or at least, you have been that girl, once or twice. When it comes to kissing, you've got the market cornered. But you may be missing out on something wilder than the hallway makeout—suspense.

Rachel took the quiz, too,
so go to www.rachelvail.com for her results!

# kiss me again

We stared into each other's eyes for a few more long seconds. He sucked in on his lips, like he wanted to taste them. I tried not to look at his lips and simultaneously tried to hold back the growing dread inside me that maybe kissing his forehead was a weird thing to do. Subtly but deeply weird. Like wearing a polo shirt buttoned all the way up.

A hint of a smile tipped up a corner of his mouth.

It occurred to me that maybe I had accidentally said the thing about the polo shirt out loud, or that maybe he could read my mind. Or, maybe, that he just wanted to smile because he was looking at me.

That thought made my fingers all go numb. They hung like sausages from my hands. I sent up a silent prayer that he would not notice them and back away, horrified, shrieking, "Ack! Sausage fingers!"

I decided to say a quick, firm *good night* so he would get the hint and leave my room before I humiliated myself further or started cracking myself up at the weirdness of this whole mess, but my mouth clearly did not get the memo because instead it just mirrored the semi-smile on Kevin's mouth.

"So . . ." he breathed.

"Mmm," I answered, meaning *mmm-hmm*, as in *yes*, like, *wow this is awkward*. But the *hmm* of the *mmm-hmm* got cut off, which made it more like a hum, more like *mmm, yes this is good*.

He reached toward my head and touched a piece of hair that had sprung out of a twist. He twirled it around his finger. Which was a problem because I am apparently allergic to Kevin Lazarus twirling a piece of my hair. It makes breathing very difficult for me. Also, retaining my coordination enough to remain standing. Also, thinking.

"I kissed George today," I blurted, surprising us both.

"Okay," Kevin said. He still kept ahold of that piece of my hair. I made sure my head stayed still so it wouldn't get yanked out of his fingers.

"At the wedding," I for some reason felt the need to add.

"I figured."

"But we're not going out or anything," I said. "Officially. Not that . . ."

"Charlie," he whispered, and just at that exact moment my knees dissolved. He caught my chin with his upturned right palm and moved it toward his face.

I felt the heat even more than the texture of his lips on mine.

My eyes closed.

I didn't think *no, no, no, I cannot be kissing this boy*.

I didn't think *wow I really like kissing Kevin Lazarus*.

I didn't, for once, think anything.

I just felt the light heat of my lips and Kevin's lips, barely but definitely, meltingly, touching.

My eyes, opening slowly, met his.

"Good night," he whispered.

"Yeah," I whispered back.

His thumb swiped lightly down my cheek before he turned around and walked down the hall. I stayed right where I was, not moving or, well, possibly swaying slightly in the swirly air currents he had caused by walking away.

When he got to his door, he turned his face partway back to me. The smile on his mouth bloomed slowly. I watched it spread across the lips I'd just been kissing and, with supreme willpower, didn't either fall down or follow him into his room to mash my face against his.

"See you in the morning," he whispered.

"Yeah."

And then, because the other choice was a Very Bad one, and my one remaining working brain cell fired, I turned around and dashed to my bed.

But I didn't close my door.

I spent the next few hours, with my heart pounding, staring at that open space, shackling my wrists with my top sheet to keep me pinned right there and warning myself that terrible fates would crash down on me if I made one move toward that open door.